B

Other Books by Jonathan Baumbach:

D-Tours

Seven Wives: a romance

Separate Hours

The Life and Times of Major Fiction

My Father More or Less

The Return of Service

Chez Charlotte and Emily

Babble

Reruns

What Comes Next

A Man to Conjure with

The Landscape of Nightmare: Studies in the Contemporary American Novel

B
a novel

by Jonathan Baumbach

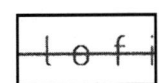

low fidelity press
new york, new york

Copyright © 2002 by Jonathan Baumbach
All rights reserved.

Low Fidelity press
P.O. Box 21930
Brooklyn, NY 11202-1930

info@lofipress.com
http://www.lofipress.com

The following sections of this novel appeared in the following publications in slightly different form: "The Reading," "Intimacy," "His View of Her View of Him," "The Blind Date," "An Annotated History of the Past," in *Boulevard*; "Lost in Eros" in *Central Park*; "Heartbreak Anonymous" in *Fiction International* (under the title "Frozen Seas"); "The History of Elegance" in *Columbia Magazine*; and "Weddings" in *WebDelSol*.

Library of Congress Cataloging-in-Publication Data

Baumbach, Jonathan.
 B : a novel / by Jonathan Baumbach.
   p. cm.
 ISBN 0-9723363-0-3
 1. Poets—Fiction. 2. Failure (Psychology)—Fiction. 3. Identity (Psychology)—Fiction. 4. Autobiography—Authorship—Fiction. I. Title.
 PS3552.A844 B15 2002
 813'.54—dc21

2002151293

Cover design by Drew Kinney
Book design by Jeff Parker

Printed in Canada.

To the memory of my parents:

Harold Baumbach (1903-2001)
Ida Baumbach (1906-2002)

If only there were a perfect moment in the book;
if only we could live in that moment,
we could begin the book again
as if we had not written it,
as if we weren't in it.

—from Mark Strand's *The Story of Our Lives*

I.	Prologue
II.	An Authorized Life
III.	The Reading
IV.	Playing the Game
V.	The Blind Date
VI.	Lost in Eros
VII.	Heartbreak Anonymous
VIII.	Obligations
IX.	Intimacy
X.	The History of Elegance
XI.	An Annotated History of the Past
XII.	Outtakes
XIII.	Weddings
XIV.	His View of Her View of Him

I. PROLOGUE

When I reached 50, turned that mortal corner, I decided it was time to tell my own story unmediated by metaphorical disguise. Mainly I was blocked on a novel I had started two years ago and needed to try something else to get out of my funk. I imagined in telling the story of my life I would rediscover pieces of myself I had lost, which might have some interest to readers who had a similar sense of incompleteness and dislocation. In the past, whenever I thought of writing a memoir, I would hear my father's ironic voice mocking my presumption.

—So you think your life is more interesting than anyone else's?

I had to find some way to silence my father's imagined objections before I could begin. If not exceptionally unusual, my life at least had been eventful. I had been married three times and in love (in the illusion of) at least seven others; I had four children; I had lived passionately (some of the time, much of it in the imagination); I had served in the army (between wars); I had written a number of books.

And if not that eventful, at least my life had been substantial and serious. Or so I believed or mostly believed or aspired to believe. It was possible that the memoir I was positioned to write was a story of self-deception. All those marriages and divorces: they were a record of disappointment and failure. I had either chosen to marry the wrong women (the roseate delusions of romantic love) or I had been too self-involved to adjust to living with another person over an extended period of time.

Well, wasn't that the point? My failures were what gave my life the shape and dazzle of fiction. I continually found new ways to deceive myself into making what turned out to be the same mistake. I had married three times to women, on the surface, considerably different from each other, though after I had lived with them for awhile they all turned out to be the same person, the female version of my semi-mad father. It was almost mystical—like some kind of damnable fate—the bizarre metamorphosis of each of my wives into the same prototypical impossible wife. How many men could boast that they had married three different female versions of their father?

II. AN AUTHORIZED LIFE

1.
Unattached for the moment, serving the indefinite life sentence of his freedom, B felt at times (not all the time) unendurably lonely. The Harts, Max and Heather, out of kindness or pity or whatever, had him over for dinner at least once a week. For reasons he didn't want to investigate, they had made looking after him during this difficult period their personal project. They were relatively new friends, had been neighbors during his most recent failed marriage. He had only known them seven years. Max was a stockbroker, who had some ties to the movie business including a West Coast apartment. Heather, after a 20-year hiatus, had gone back to school to get a Ph.D. in clinical psychology. They were both lively people, though it took B almost a year to warm up to them. He had never imagined in the early days of the relationship that he'd become such inseparable friends with this hermetic couple.

Now he spent so much time with the Harts, it was as if the three of them had become an entity. Whenever Heather hugged him—usually coming and going—he felt a rush of pleasure that made him want to run for his life. He imagined a secret (sexual) understanding between them, an understanding that they were both too sane and mature to take to the next stage.

The Harts did whatever they could to ease his bouts of sadness, which came and went but rarely stayed away for long. When he told them he was blocked as a writer, Heather insisted she knew the way out. The thing to do was to write his autobiography for which, she supposed, he had a ready-made story. B enthused over the suggestion but privately rejected the idea. Nonfiction, because of its implicit presumption, had never seemed to him quite credible. Still, wanting to please Heather, he sat down at his computer that night and wrote an opening sentence to a memoir, a sentence he worked and reworked until it was dense beyond comprehension. Though unusable, it was an irrevocable beginning. He had a project now between the other things he did to fill his day—the exercises for his back, the pursuit of love, the caretaking of his parents, the reading and unreading of his unfinished novel.

Heather and Max had given him sanction to tell his story.

Max had to go to LA on business and he was trying to convince Heather to join him for the week. It would mean missing two classes and she said she would think it over.

—Why don't you come too? he said to B.

B said he didn't know what he'd do without the two of them for a whole week, but that he had just started this memoir they had assigned him.

—Give me a couple days to mull it over, he said. He knew he wouldn't go but he wanted the possibility, or the illusion of the possibility kept open.

Heather, for her own reasons, also decided not to go with Max. When she called to ask him to dinner on Sunday, he said he had a prior engagement, which was a rehearsed lie.

—You always come here Sunday night, Heather said. How can you possibly have another engagement?

—Well, I'm not feeling too well, he said. My back has been bothering me.

She laughed at him. —I'll expect you at seven, she said. And bring a red wine if you have something available. I love the wines you bring.

He arrived at ten minutes after eight, got a sixty-five dollar ticket for easing through a stop sign on the way, pulled something in his back getting out of the car after driving around for 20 minutes looking for a place to park. He was severely bent over when Heather answered the door to let him in.

—I don't know that this is such a good idea, he said, stumbling by her, avoiding a welcoming hug.

—What is it? she said, following him onto the screened-in porch where they generally had their pre-dinner drinks. —You think I'm going to seduce you, is that what it is? Not to worry.

—You're embarrassing me, B said.

She went into the kitchen, leaving him to fend for himself. There was a fifth of Jameson's on the table, a bucket of ice, a pitcher of ice water, a bottle of seltzer and three glasses. There was also a pate with a bite out of it, bordered by a circle of Carr's mini water crackers.

—If you're having a drink, make me one too, she called from the kitchen.

He poured two glasses of whiskey, added water to one and soda to the other and delivered them to the kitchen. Heather was smoking a cigarette and stirring something in a pot.

—Hey, I've never seen you smoke before, he said.

Heather stubbed out the cigarette. —I don't smoke around Max, she said. Actually I stopped smoking nine years ago.

—Don't start again on my account, he said.

—Aren't you being just a bit presumptuous? she said, turning her attention to something at the stove.

—I was joking, he said, not sure how to take her rebuke. I didn't think your smoking had anything to do with me.

An awkward silence followed in which she seemed to contrive busyness in order to avoid looking at him. After a suitable hiatus, he excused himself and accompanied the drink he had been nursing back to the porch. He had never seen Heather like this. His evenings with Max and Heather had generally been high-spirited and playful, each of them inspiring the other two to their most witty and likable portrayals of self.

After some minutes of trying unsuccessfully to figure out what was going on, he went back into the kitchen. He was carrying a plate of three mini crackers smeared with paté as a truce offering to Heather. She was sitting at the kitchen table smoking a cigarette and drinking what looked like a vodka tonic in a tall narrow glass.

—Would you believe it, she said without looking up, I've forgotten how to cook.

—I doubt that, he said. You're one of the best cooks I know.

—Dinner will be served as soon as I get up, she announced.

On her feet, her balance seemed precarious and she followed the contour of the worktable—set up as an island in the center of the room—over to the stove. She handed him a bottle of wine to open, the Zaca Mesa cabernet he had brought as a gift. Once the dinner was on the table and they were seated—she in her usual chair, B in Max's place—she seemed to brighten, to become momentarily her old self.

—I want to hear all about your memoir, she said.

—There's nothing to tell at this point, he said. I haven't settled on a strategy for it yet.

She lifted her fork—she had eaten very little, had mostly moved her food around—and pointed it at him.

—Forget strategy, she said. Just make it truthful.

Her remark annoyed him. —Do you always know what the truth is, Heather?

—Always, she said, sticking her tongue out at him.

She resumed looking disappointedly at her food.

—Tell me about your childhood. You had one, didn't you?

—I had two or three childhoods, he said. I've been looking at old photos as a way of sorting out the past. In none of the pictures I located was I smiling. Heather's eyes went in and out of focus.

—I'm sorry to hear that, she said. I had a happy childhood. All my friends had happy childhoods. I feel so bad for you it makes me want to cry.

—Eat something, Heather, he said.

Heather put a small piece of chicken in her mouth and chewed on it as if it were work that required all her powers of concentration. —The food is good, she said. You don't always know how things will turn out. I'm feeling odd.

She got up slowly, smiled at him as an afterthought, and walked away from the table. A few minutes later she called something to him from upstairs, something which sounded like, –Don't wait for me, but it was possible he misunderstood and she was asking him for some assistance. She had been too drunk to eat, which was uncharacteristic. He had never seen her this out of it before and he thought if she were sick the least he could do was help her through it.

So he went looking for her, went up the stairs calling to her, not wanting to invade her privacy without permission. He heard what sounded like a hair dryer—it could also have been the purring of a cat—and he followed the sound to the master bedroom. Heather was sprawled across the bed, her feet hanging over one side. He straightened her out, removed her shoes, and turned to leave.

–Where you going? she asked, her head popping up. This is not me.

–It's time for me to go home, he said. When she didn't respond he went downstairs and recovered his jacket from the hall closet.

–Go home here, she called from her room.

–I don't know what you mean, he said.

–I can't hear you, she called back. Did you say something? Did he say something?

He grudgingly reclimbed the winding stairway and lounged in the doorway of the Harts' bedroom. Her eyes were closed and he waited for some indication that she was awake before announcing again his intention to take off. When she opened her eyes and saw him or perhaps saw his looming shadow in the doorway, she let out a gasp.

–Come in if you're coming in, she said. She patted a space on the bed next to her.

–I'm going now, Heather, he said.

–Have a safe trip, she said....You've always led me to believe that you were besotted by my charms. Was that a
calculated deception?

He found himself laughing or trying not to laugh, which amounted to the same thing. –You're a funny woman, Heather.

–I just want to make it clear that I was not asking you to share my bed, she said. I was thinking you might like to stay in one of the spare bedrooms and drive home in the morning. He glanced at his watch which was hard to read in the dim hallway. One of the hands was between the eleven and the twelve. The other was either behind it or illegible in the dim light.

—Get some sleep, he said, meaning sleep it off.

—Just because I had too much to drink and retched on my shoes doesn't make me a bad person, she said. If you feel you have to go, you have my permission to leave. Go.

Her abrupt dismissal caused him to hesitate. —Heather, I want to say that your friendship and support have been important to me during what has been, as you well know, a difficult period.

—Is that right? she said. Well your friendship has been important to me too. I have a confession I want to make to you. Will you hear my confession, friend?

Of course B didn't want to hear it, it was the last thing he wanted to hear, but how could he walk away after saying what he had. He found a hard wooden chair and pulled it up a half a foot from the bed. There was an odd noise in the room with them which he recognized momentarily as Heather sobbing, fighting herself to speak.

—This is between us, she said. Max doesn't know anything about this and I don't want him ever to know. Give me your promise that he'll never know.

—I can't control what Max knows or doesn't know, he said. If you tell me something you don't want repeated, I'll respect that.

She laughed. —I feel as if I ought to ask you for a blood oath whatever that is. This business has been driving me bananas. Give me your word you'll not say anything.

—If you can't trust me, don't tell me, he said.

—That's fair, she said. Or is it? About sixteen years ago, it's more like seventeen now, I was in therapy briefly with this guy who had a practice in the neighborhood. I had a panic attack while I was walking to the market and I saw his shingle and I knocked at his door. Anyway, he was very kind and patient and he talked me through my anxiety. After that we set up a once a week session to explore the causes of my panic attacks. From our first meeting on, he was more like a friend than a therapist. I remember telling him how comfortable I felt in his presence. It was the same for him with me, he said. He had just separated from his wife and I was going through a sticky patch with Max. He was very easy to talk to, he was, and I badly needed someone to talk to.

So it was not about him, this confession, which was both a relief and a disappointment. Heather had another crying jag at this point and much of the rest of her story had to be pieced together to be made coherent. The gist of it was she had been having a secret affair with this man for 17 years for which she felt terrible guilt but (had B got that right?) they had only slept together, rather unsatisfactorily as it turned out, one time. The affair consisted in meeting secretly, usually once a week, to discuss the need to keep matters secret and whatever else came up. There had been nothing but talk and some hand holding after the first go.

–Don't look so astonished, she said. I don't understand it myself. So? She took his hand and he moved from his chair to the edge of the bed.

–What do you want me to tell you? he said. You're a smart person. You know what you need to do.

–I don't, she said. Tell me what I should do.

The intimacy her confession implied elated B, overrode any discomfort he felt at being alone in the bedroom with an attractive woman who was married to a friend.

–Do you love this man you've been seeing? he asked. The question produced an extended silence.

–I must, don't you think? she said at last. Why else would I keep seeing him? That wasn't the answer he was hoping to get.

–I don't see how you've kept this from Max. Max must know something.

–You think so? I have the idea that Max doesn't want to know. Sometimes I think Max is having an affair and is using my infidelity as his justification. If you were Max, would you want to know that your wife was involved in a long term relationship with another man? The question touched an unhealed sore.

–You have to stop this once a week nonsense, he said. And I think you should tell Max. She was silent again and he sensed her annoyance with his answer.

—I know it's hard, he said, but you're a strong person, Heather.
—Fuck you, she said.

When she released his hand, he got up from his perch on the bed. His back was hurting and he had difficulty straightening up.

—I meant the fuck you in a positive way, she said. It would be much appreciated if you stayed the night. When I get into a panic, I need to have someone I can trust around.

—

When B (the hero of my memoir) finally confronts his wife about the man she has been spending so much time with and asks if she is having an affair, she says no, it is just a friendship and of course they are working together, collaborating on this children's book. The answer comforts him and he lets matters ride another week. And then another. The next time he confronts her, she breaks down and cries.

—

He said or was thinking of saying that he would stay until she fell asleep when Max phoned from Los Angeles. While they were talking, he tried to slip quietly out of the room but he stepped on an errant shoe and turned his ankle, holding on to the wall to keep from falling. His back was throbbing. He tried not to listen, but of course he couldn't avoid hearing their conversation. They talked for fifteen minutes or more, just chat for the most part, a sharing of the events of their time apart. They were so easy with one another, so respectful, so affectionate, so intimate it was as though they were taunting him. If he were ever to imagine an ideal couple on the page, the Harts would be his example. Heather mentioned that he had come to dinner but not that he was still there, not that he was in the bedroom with her, his back against the wall, trying with minimal success to tune out their conversation. He felt further compromised by her implicit lie.

—Why didn't you tell him I was here, he complained when she was off the phone, but of course he knew the answer and so did she and so there was nothing to be said.

2.
When B was five years old, he had gotten hit by a car, causing a mild concussion and some residual anxiety. He seemed "nervous" for a number of years after that, which was attributed to the trauma of his brush with death. He dredges up the memory of his accident—not that he has ever completely forgotten it—when he finds himself lying in bed, their legs entangled, next to his friend's wife.

He thinks of himself perpetually caught in the lights of a car, trying to decide which way to tumble to avoid being hit, paralyzed by indecision.

Even as an adult, he felt vulnerable to the unexpected. He could never wholly shake the feeling that some unseen danger awaited him around the next blind turn. As a way of averting disaster, he tended to anticipate bad news. Still, he was unprepared for a call from Max virtually demanding that he come down to his office that afternoon for a talk.

–What's this about? he asked him. Max mumbled something about not wanting to discuss it on the phone. Before going off to see Max, he called Heather to get some inkling of what awaited him. Another piece of unexpected news: Heather had no idea that Max had made this appointment with him. She had, she told him, considered ending the relationship with the man she had been having the non-sexual affair with for seventeen years, but she hadn't told Max about it, not yet.

–So, she said, the reason Max wants to see you can't have anything to do with me. I suppose you wouldn't want to tell me afterwards what it was about.

–If I betrayed Max's confidence, he said, how could you trust me not to betray yours?

–I was teasing you, she said. Don't you know when you're being teased? Still, it's a strange thing for Max to do, isn't it? Has he done something like this before?

–Done something like what before? he asked.

—You know, she said. Don't give me a hard time, okay? And don't ask me to ask Max because Max doesn't know I know he set up this meeting with you. All these secrets are making me crazy.

B thought of postponing his meeting with Max but he was too distracted to do much else so he procrastinated, worked up some low level anxiety, until it was time for him to leave. Despite what Heather had said, he was all but sure that this meeting had something to do with his having spent the night at their place when Max was away. Why else had Max been so grim over the phone?

Max took him to lunch at an exotic vegetarian restaurant called the Sensuous Palate without even asking him if the choice was acceptable.

—I'm thinking of becoming a vegetarian, Max announced as if that explained something.

He had to wait until the meal was almost over for Max's bombshell. —I want you to put yourself in my shoes for a minute, he said. That's something a writer, someone who uses his imagination for a living, ought to be expert at, right?

B was careful with his response, continued to suspect Max was playing some kind of cat-and-mouse game with him.

—I'm probably the exception that proves the rule, he said. I never put on other people's shoes. I have enough trouble getting my own on the appropriate feet.

—Good, Max said, an indication that he wasn't listening. Unlike you, I'm someone who's always believed in the sanctity of marriage. In the 24 years Heather and I have been together, there have only been two lapses. That's not perfect, but certainly from what I hear better than average. A week ago if I made this confession to you, I would have said there had been only one lapse in twenty-four years.

—Something happened during your most recent trip to California.

Max put his hands over his face. —Mea culpa, he mumbled.

B gave an inward (unheard, he hoped) sigh of relief. This wasn't about him apparently, though he remained wary. —Did you at least enjoy it? he asked.

—Hated it, Max said, a nervous laugh escaping. I can't even

tell you how it happened. Gail's husband had left her and she was feeling down and I was trying to make her feel better. She worked for me on a picture I had a producer credit on a couple years ago and we had remained friends. Anyway, it was probably a one night thing. I don't see it happening again.

–You don't have to justify yourself to me, B said.

–I feel terrible about what happened, Max said. This isn't me. And I haven't told you the most disturbing thing. The girl, she thinks she's in love with me and that this is going to be some kind of permanent thing with us. I told her I have no intention of leaving Heather, but she won't believe me. It's a mess. The kid's in a very vulnerable phase.

–What do you want me to tell you?

–How would you handle it if you were in my shoes? Max asked.

–I'd fuck things up, he said. The thing to do right away is to tell Heather.

–That's the one thing I can't do, Max said. When I had my other lapse—this was about 18 years ago—Heather forgave me, but she said if it happened again it was over between us.

–You don't think Heather would forgive you? You've been together 24 years.

–Two months from today is our twenty-fifth anniversary, Max said. Why does she need to know? And the last thing I need is to be forgiven, for God's sake. Being forgiven is one of the worst burdens I can think of. Anyhow, would you want to know if you were her?

B didn't answer. He took a bite of his apricot and bamboo tart and savored the experience with insufficient pleasure. He didn't think he could fit into Max's shoes and Heather's shoes at the same time.

–You want me to tell her, don't you? Max said. You want to see Heather hurt and our marriage in distress. If Heather and I broke up, you could step in and comfort her. That's what you want, isn't it?

3.

B didn't go to the Harts for dinner the following Sunday, made some excuse about having to see an old friend who was visiting from out of town. It seemed to be a mutual decision since Heather, who had picked up, said they had been remiss in not letting him know they were going to be away for the weekend. He was fond of Heather and Max and felt aggrieved his friendship with them had taken this awkward turn. He took time off from his memoir to write them a joint letter, which of course he couldn't send because it implicitly violated each of their confidences.

The following week B was not invited to Sunday dinner or at least not explicitly invited. After not seeing Max and Heather for three weeks, he called to say he wanted to take them to dinner at Cucina, which was a place the Harts tended to go on celebratory occasions. Max answered, sounded glad to hear his voice, said Heather was out and that he would call back after he spoke to her. B's curiosity got the better of his judgment.

—Did you tell her about your second lapse? he asked.

—That was bad advice you gave me, buddy, Max said. Because I was foolish enough to listen to you, matters are a little dicey at home right now. Look, I'll call you back when Heather gets in. Max called back a few hours later to say they would have to pass on his dinner invitation. —Heather doesn't want to have anything to do with you for the time being.

The news surprised and pained him. B tried to imagine his offense, imagined a variety of possible offenses and regretted them all. —What's this about? he asked.

—I haven't a clue, Max said. Even if I knew, Heather has the right to represent her position in her own words. Don't you think so?

—Would you put her on the phone?

Max was gone for a few minutes and B rehearsed his opening line to Heather, a running gag they had between them, but it was Max who returned to the phone. —She's too pissed to talk to you, he said.

For the next few days, B knew in effect what it was like to be banished from Paradise with no hope of return. The two people in the world he felt closest to had, for no fault he was willing to acknowledge, turned against him.

—

I have to admit at this point that I had my doubts as to whether this was the right episode with which to begin the book.

—

B's wife, which is how he still thinks of her, calls to ask him to pay the gas bill at his former house. While she has him on the phone, he asks her if she thinks the Harts are reliable people.
 —I haven't seen them since our breakup, she says. Have you been seeing them? I always liked him better than her. There's something about Heather that tends to put me off.

4.
After a month of banishment passed, B ran into Heather at the local D'Agostino's. She was coming down the very aisle he turned up and he stopped in his tracks the instant he saw her. There was no way to avoid being seen so he affected a casual pose, waiting for Heather to make the first gesture. She had been studying a shelf of floor waxes so it took a moment for her to notice him.
 —Where have you been keeping yourself, stranger? she said, approaching like the car he had been unable to escape in his dreams. She gave him a hug that lasted it seemed a couple of beats longer than convention required. She waited for him to finish his shopping and they walked out of the supermarket together. He carried one of Heather's supermarket bags for her along with his own small pickings. He rarely bought more than three or four items at a time when he shopped.
 —I'm glad we're friends again, he said.
 —What do you mean again? she said. When did we stop being friends?

—Well, he said but then he decided not to press the issue.

—How's the autobiography coming? Heather asked. Have you found a strategy? You see I remembered what you said.

They stopped at Purity, a local diner, for a cup of coffee.

—My strategy is to start with the present, he said, and associate from it into past events with similar configurations. Or not.

—Whatever, Heather said. She stared off into space as if she were dissecting his remarks though perhaps she was musing about something else altogether. The coffee was terrible as usual, but its familiarity had a kind of nurturing effect. It was the essence of all the bad burned coffee he ever had in diners everywhere. It was like mother's milk, he thought, though as he had never been nursed (his mother had tried, she said, and failed) he could only imagine that mother's milk, whatever the taste, was similarly comforting. He found himself staring at Heather's breasts.

—You'll be happy to hear I've taken your advice, she said. It's a great relief, I'll tell you, not to have to carry that burden around with me.

—You told Max? he asked.

—Better than that, she said, looking around the restaurant to see if there was anyone she knew. I've created a situation where there's no longer any need for confession. I think you understand what I'm saying.

He was uneasy with the confidentiality of Heather's tone. The sure way to kill a friendship was to be given glimpses of a secret life that didn't and couldn't concern him. To change the subject, he told her how much their friendship, the dinners at their place, had meant to him over the past few months.

She laughed at his earnestness. —Tell me something I don't know, she said.

—I would if I could think of something, he said.

After they had finished with their coffees—the waitress had filled his cup twice—B walked Heather from the restaurant to her door.

—I'm glad I ran into you, she said, hugging him again. That was fun. We should do this more often.

He watched her climb the steps to her brownstone, feeling

oddly embarrassed as if their incidental meeting, their going for coffee together, his escorting her home, represented some undefined violation. Not only that but it felt like a violation he had committed many times before. When she was gone he felt a sense of loss which surely had more to do with something in his past than with Heather going inside.

B surveyed his feelings on the way home. He was not romantically involved with Heather, he decided, and had never been. She was a smart, slightly crazy, sexy woman and he liked her. But he was also aware that he wanted something from her, wanted her—it was hard to define exactly what—to...love him. Was that what it was? Wasn't that pathetic!

So when Heather called to invite B to have lunch with her the following Thursday, he offered some involved probably unconvincing lie as to why he couldn't make it.

—If you won't come, Heather said, I'm going to end up visiting Roger again. Do you want that to happen?

Surely those weren't the only two choices, he thought, but he withheld the remark. —Roger is your heroin habit, he said. And I'm your methadone cure.

—That's not so far from the truth, she said.

He regretted turning down Heather's request—you don't turn down a friend who's asking for help—and he called back the next day to say he had gotten out of his prior appointment and was now available for lunch. The first time he called he got their answering machine and left no message. When he tried again an hour later, Max picked up. As an improvisatory move, he reissued his invitation to take the two of them out to dinner some Sunday. Max said they would prefer to stay in and barbecue and why didn't he join them this Sunday like old times.

So his relationship with the Harts had turned another corner. He had been restored to their good graces. "Paradise regained!" he wrote in his journal. Yet the sense of loss he had felt a few weeks ago when they had cut him off lingered. It was further exacerbated by an unreasoning anger he felt toward Max and Heather as a couple, as an entity that excluded him from the intimate world they shared. It was all so familiar what had happened, the twists and turns of his relationship with the Harts, it was as if he had been rehearsing in variation the same unwatchable movie all his life.

—

B's mother dotes on him, yet his father's needs, which are various and unending, almost always have priority. Do I have that right?

—

B called the Harts Saturday morning and begged out of his appointment for Sunday dinner. Heather tried to cajole him into changing his mind. —It won't be the same without you, she said. You have to come. Tell whoever it is you're seeing that you have a prior unbreakable commitment to us. You know we love you. You have to come.

It was as if the sirens were singing to him and he was lashed to the boat. —I appreciate what you're saying, he said, but I can't do it this Sunday.

—You're a shit, she said, laughing.

And though he knew it was true, he liked himself better for refusing her.

—

In truth I had gone back and forth on B's decision. Either way was problematic. Even if he went to the Hart's barbecue, his relationship with them would be irrevocably altered by the events preceding the renewed invitation.

—

You weren't quite alive, B told himself, unless you surprised at least once in a while that unseen imaginary observer watching you perform. On Sunday morning he called the Harts and got Max. After they joked a bit—their usual by-play—he told Max he could see them tonight for dinner if the invitation was still good.

—You come over to dinner, said Max, and I'll forgive you everything.

III. THE READING

B travels by train to give a reading of his poems at an obscure liberal arts college in southern Pennsylvania. His mint green Saab, which has been virtually the shell on his back, has come down with a case of transmission failure the morning of the trip. Worse news, it is his habit to believe, lies ahead. When his wife left him fifteen months ago to run off with a criminal lawyer who also happened to be a friend, his life, which had been finely tuned for years, fell abruptly and perhaps irremediably into screeching disarray.

When the train arrives at the college station twenty minutes late, no one is on the platform to meet him. What's that all about? Already nightfall, the dark platform seems a deserted street in the middle of nowhere. Has he been lured here only to be abandoned in darkness? The tips of B's fingers are chilled, almost numb from the cold. He paces the platform, his hands in the pockets of his leather jacket, and waits. It is unrewarding activity, pacing and waiting, reminding him of the bad luck he is embarrassed to believe in and can't seem to shake.

He approaches the grizzled ticketseller, who withholds speech as if there were no getting it back once given away. Still, if you ask the right questions, he has always believed, the information you're after will work its way through the cracks. The college, he interpolates from the ticketseller's grunts and headshakes, is too far away to walk. There are no cabs available after six thirty. The station's two public phones have been out of order for months. After awhile another train arrives. B, who has nothing better to do, meets it as if he were meeting himself. Two people get off at the dark and deserted station. One is a woman he knows slightly, a poet he met two years ago at a writer's conference and fell in love with at sight. He has not seen her since.

When he introduces himself (she doesn't remember having met him), the woman, Y, assumes B is a representative of the college there to meet her, a delusion she holds on to even after he explains that he too has been stood up. When he tells her of their mutual predicament, she reproaches him in a graceful way on his failures as a host.

—You must learn to plan ahead, she says. Not everything we do works out as we intend it. He acknowledges the wisdom of her remarks, suggests they walk toward the college with the hope of promoting a ride along the way. She will stay at the station, she says, and wait for them to come to her. It is her method in all things to let others come to her.

What can B do but wait with her. —I can't leave you, he says, a remark which earns him a hit-and-run kiss on the cheek.

—Never? she asks.

He wonders at that moment if there weren't something fateful about them meeting this way at the deserted college station. —It does stand to reason, doesn't it? B says, that the college, having planned on our being there, will send someone to claim us. The remark earns him a second kiss, this one passed from her fingers to his cheek. They sit for a while on one of the dark platform's two backless stone benches, leaning in to each other to keep the cold wind from taking residence between them.

—I do remember you now, she says.

They talk about walking up and down to get warm or going inside the building to escape the wind. Ways of warming themselves is not their only subject. He is surprised when he puts his arm around her and she cuddles into his shoulder, as much surprised at his own gesture as at hers. His lost and barely remembered feelings for this woman revisit uninvited. Sensation returns to the tips of his fingers.

B

When they stand up to go inside, she lets herself be kissed. She covers his mouth with her hand when he tries or seems about to try to explain himself. It is not as if he had anything to say that had not been heard. It is uncomfortable inside the small waiting room, airless and overbright, radiators wheezing like slumbering drunks. In the light, he discovers that she is not the person he thought she was, not the one he fell in love with at sight. This unlooked for discovery leaves him emotionally bereft as if his most passionate feelings had remained on the platform without him.

He doesn't tell her that she is the wrong one. They sit like strangers now, slightly apart, each reading a book of the other's poems. The taste of her tongue, the weight of her head on his shoulder, are barely a memory. And this is the way they are, lost and found, when the awkwardly shy Assistant Professor who had been sent to pick them up makes his apologetic appearance.

—Can you believe it? I couldn't find the station, he tells them.

The Assistant Professor drives them toward the college in his cluttered brown and green station wagon, the seats and floor decorated with debris, old newspapers and magazines, loose Pampers, broken plastic toys, almost every surface occupied. They run out of gas before they arrive and their surrogate host, who is prepared for such emergencies, hurries off with a one gallon can under his arm, telling them not to worry that he's done this before.

Moments after he leaves, a white late-model oversized American car drives up alongside their beached whale. A white-haired man in formal clothes, a trustee perhaps, sticks his head out the window and asks them if they would like a ride to the college. B, who has no trust in the Assistant Professor, accepts immediately (though his door won't open), but the woman in back (the one he's fallen in and out of love with in the past hour) says the appropriate thing to do would be to wait for their driver to return. B argues his case, but the woman won't be dissuaded from what she knows to be the right course.

—I can't leave her, he explains to the trustee, who drives off without them.

—When you say that, she tells him when they're alone again, it makes me want to cry.

The Assistant Professor returns, feeds the empty tank, starts the car, and they drive to the college without further mishap. Except they arrive on campus ten minutes after the reading is scheduled and they find themselves locked out of the appointed building, Affect Hall. What's with this college? Even if they get the building open (and the Assistant Professor has, with that intent in mind, gone off to find a key) where will an audience come from? There is no one else, no small clique of English majors, waiting to get in. At that point, B realizes that he has left his overnight bag at the train station. The only thing he can do, which is of little practical value, is imagine himself calling the station and asking the uncommunicative ticketseller to put his bag in a safe place for him until he can manage his return.

A security guard unlocks the building from inside. Momentarily, they are milling around in a small auditorium, the other poet, Y, holding his hand in a secretive way. An audience of five assembles itself. The poet asks his companion whether she'd like to go first or second. She has been drinking from a flask and is slightly befuddled.

—What are my other choices? she asks.

The chairman of the English Department, who wears black glasses, arrives to introduce the readers, or so B understands the man's role when he takes the podium. The chairman, who is blind, reads his prepared text with his fingers. His written introduction seems for the first ten minutes or so elaborate and obscure. Neither B nor the faded beauty Y is mentioned by name. What's it all about? The blind chairman goes on and on as if it were not an introduction at all but a paper elaborating a theory of language.

—Language is the whim of silence, says the speaker. Panic moves B to get up from his seat in the front row and look around the room. Are the others in the audience as astonished at the blind chairman's performance as he is?

—Sit down, Y whispers at him.

—Don't you find this strange? he asks her. She puts a finger over her lips, splitting a smile. When he sits down, she puts her lips over his to preserve his unhappy silence.

When the introduction goes into its second hour most of the small audience leaves. Only B and Y and the chairman's hearing-impaired wife continue their vigil. The Assistant Professor comes running down the aisle, waving his arms.

—What's the problem?

—There's been a mix-up, he says. The Broadsnore Lecture is in here. You people are supposed to be in another room altogether. Y insists on staying to the end of the lecture and B is conflicted on whether to leave or not.

—Come with me, he pleads.

—It's not right to walk out on him, she says.

B follows the Assistant Professor into a somewhat smaller room down the hall. There is an overflow crowd, as it turns out, waiting for him. They stamp their feet in welcome on his appearance at the podium.

—You can't believe what I went through to get here, he says. That brings a laugh. It falls to the Assistant Professor to introduce him.

—I don't have to tell you how privileged we are to have this man with us today, he starts out, an inappropriate remark that speaks to B's unacknowledged secret self.

The fulsome introduction continues. B is pictured as a defender of the defenseless, a man willing to take up causes so unpopular no one else in his right mind would dare touch them. What's going on? The praise touches him almost to the point of tears. How does this bumptious Assistant Professor know so much about him, he wonders. It is as if he were introducing some figure of national prominence and not a relatively obscure poet known, if at all, for his uncompromising difficulty. And then his name is mentioned (though it is not exactly his name) to standing applause. He has been mistaken for someone else, a trial lawyer (and former basketball great) who has a predilection for representing only the blatantly guilty. At first B plans to deny that he is the famous lawyer they've been waiting for, but then he thinks, Well, maybe there's a more graceful way to avoid the embarrassment of this foolish mistake. Besides he has never had a crowd this large come to hear him. An ambiguous disclaimer might be sufficient.

—I am not the man you think I am, he says, which invites further applause. Your support and affection have made this moment possible. There can be no justice without a constituency that acknowledges the possibility of justice. Having run out of platitudes, he waits for inspiration.

—Why do I do what I do? he asks. The answer sits waiting for him. Because if I don't, no one else will. The audience offers him a standing ovation. The back door opens and Y, looking tired and lost, slips into the room.

—To give you a sense of who I am, he says, I want to read you some poems by a poet who I sometimes think speaks for me. The audience clears its collective throat. Y alone applauds.

B reads his poems for twenty minutes to mumbled confusion. The audience has a glazed look on its collective face when he stops.

—Are there any questions? he asks. An older woman in the third row has her hand up in a determined way and he nods in her direction. She turns to look behind her before speaking.

—I don't normally ask questions in public, she says in a histrionic voice. This is what I want to know. Would you defend someone who would kill his own mother?

—If I don't, who will? he says. Next question.

—If you didn't, another headline seeker would, a voice shouts out.

B points to a young girl in the back.

—In your opinion, what is the worst crime a person could commit? she asks in a quivering voice. —And would you defend such a person?

B repeats the question for those of the audience who might not have heard it. —The worst crime, huh? The worst crime is the betrayal of self. The worst crime is the betrayal of love. The worst crime is any crime that has a victim. Such crimes are unforgivable and must be defended.

—Yeah, the audience chants in one voice.

A middle-aged man with alcoholic's eyes asks, —Have you ever committed an unforgivable crime yourself?

—Yes, says B.

—Are you willing to say what that crime was?

—No, I'm not.

—Animals have rights too, a woman in the fifth row says in

an angry voice. —Do you think the killing of an innocent animal should be a capital offense? I want a yes or no answer.

—Yes or no, says B, playing for the easy laugh. Depends on how innocent the animal is.

The animal woman gets up and walks out of the room in an earnest huff. Her departure, or perhaps B's answer, freezes the crowd. B waits patiently for another hand to rise. Y has the next question.

—Were the poems you read, she asks, written by one of your unforgivable clients?

—We are all forgivable, I hope, says B.

The Assistant Professor ends the question period by stepping in front of B and inviting everyone to a reception in a lounge downstairs—wine without chemical additives and lo-fat cheese—where the audience will be given opportunity to meet face to face with their celebrated guest. B, weary of the imposture, looks for a way out, takes Y's hand and pulls her inside a stairwell away from the crowd.

—What do you say we pursue justice elsewhere, he says. He expects resistance and is almost disappointed when she says,

—Where can we go?

—Let's just wait here until the crowd disperses, he says, realizing in the next moment that it is not Y whose hand he has taken but someone else, the woman who had been standing next to Y, the one concerned with meting out justice to animal slayers.

Y finds him with the animal woman before B can excuse himself to leave. She calls him by his presumed name, tells him (eyeing the other woman) that his fans are waiting for him in the lounge.

What fans are those? B makes a whirlwind tour of the lounge, pressing flesh like a politician, dispensing whatever wisdom the oiled tongue has to offer.

After the reception there is another party then dinner, then another party. Between the first and third party he has lost Y with whom he has again fallen in love. Anyway it is late and he is slightly drunk and very tired so he goes to the room they've assigned him in the Alumni House to take a nap or bed down for the night, however it goes.

When he opens the door to the room he assumes is his, Room 2 according to the number on his key, he senses that something is amiss. Though the lock on the door answers to his key, there is an intruder in the bed sleeping soundlessly. It is the second thing he notices, the impostor in his bed, the first is the neatly folded pile of clothes on the chair across the room. B leaves silently, takes his outrage and exhaustion with him, sits on the stairs in the hall with his head in his hands. What can he do? He gets a brainstorm, decides to try the doors to the other rooms. There is a couple in Room 1 fucking in a dispirited way and B's head is in and out before the couple, who turn to stare at him, have time to ask him what he wants. Room 3 resists his key. Room 4, his last hope for sanctuary, is unlocked and unoccupied. B slips into the room like a thief. He locks the door, pulls off his shoes without undoing the laces, and falls into bed—perhaps even falls asleep.

Next thing he knows someone is knocking on the door. Then he hears a key in the lock and the door click open. A man with a cane walks haltingly toward the bed. The figure takes off its clothes, piles them neatly on the floor and slides under the covers next to him.

—There's someone here, B says in a choked voice. The intruder raises his head, looks directly at B—their faces are no more than six inches apart—but seems not to see him. The man is asleep and snoring softly before B can protest again. He imagines himself climbing out of bed and reclaiming his shoes, a gesture he repeats over and over again, waking hours later from this dream to find a heavy arm sprawled possessively across his chest.

B slips off the bed, searches the floor for his shoes, escapes the room on his hands and knees. Y is in the hall, standing with her back to him, smoking a cigarette.

—You missed a great party, she says when he touches her shoulder.

When she turns he notices an ugly purple bruise under her right eye.

—What happened? he asks her.

—Nothing, she says, averting her eyes. Nothing worth talking about. She takes a pair of sunglasses from her purse and puts them on.

—Did they give you a room? he asks.

—Better than that, she says. I have the keys to a station wagon parked outside that we can take to the station. The thing is, I can't leave with you....And don't say what I think you're going to say.

—I'll wait until you're ready to leave, he says.

—Look it's a long story, Y says, but I promised to stay with the Assistant Professor just until he gets on his feet. His wife and children left him nine days ago and he's in a bad state, suicidal, needy and potentially violent.

The news troubles B but he says nothing more about it, waits his occasion. In the car, in the passenger seat, just as Y is about to start the engine, he has an urge to put his head in her lap, which is what he does. They kiss twice before moving to the back of the station wagon.

—You never said anything, she says. It is morning, the back door of the wagon is opened. The sudden light disturbs their sleep, discovers them in disarray, B's pants bunched at the ankles, Y's bra perched on a stack of American Scholar magazines like a huddled bird. A small crowd of onlookers makes its presence felt.

After that, the despondent Assistant Professor, full of mock bravado, traces of tears glazing his glasses, drives them to the station.

—I can't leave him like this, Y says to B when they park.

Leave him, B wants to say, but instead leaves the arena of the car himself. —I'll wait for you inside the station, he says to Y. She nods to him in uncommitted acknowledgment. He discovers his overnight case sitting in the waiting room and he picks it up and puts it on his lap, reclaims his former life.

According to the schedule in his jacket pocket the next train for New York City comes and goes in nine minutes. The one after that is three hours and twenty minutes down the road. Five minutes pass and Y is still in the station wagon locked in conversation with the aggrieved Assistant Professor. B worries that Y won't get back in time to make the train. When he looks over his shoulder to see if Y is on her way, the brown and green wagon is no longer on vigil outside. B rushes out to look for Y just as he hears the train huffing carelessly toward the station.

Y's undeniable absence echoes through the parking lot. He has lost her again. It is always the case with him: every loss seems the same loss, the first loss, the only loss. His first love was a woman he met at a mixer in his freshman year at Columbia. He betrayed her or she him. He no longer remembers.

B rushes back to board the train, unaware in his haste that the train he boards is actually coming from where he means to go.

B is dozing at a window seat unaware that he is heading toward Ohio and points west when someone slides lightly into the seat next to him. Her perfume is familiar, so is the feel of her arm on his shoulder.

—You left without me, she whispers, after all your promises. That's hard to forgive. She presents him with a ghostly peck on the cheek, the bare touch of her lips.

The opening phrase of a poem forms itself in his mind. I sensed the sky closing like the door of an abandoned....He acknowledges her reproach with a nod and closes his eyes to the unfamiliar countryside at the window—a field of motionless brown and white cows with a ramshackle red barn in the distance, a landscape absent from his history until this moment—now edging irreversibly away into the past.

Will she be there, he wonders, and will it matter, when in the course of things he finds the will or the courage or whatever it takes to look back?

IV. PLAYING THE GAME

1.
I sat down in front of my computer with the idea of getting the imagined world into motion again, a new story or perhaps another chapter for my memoir if that was how it shook out. Aside from completing my Christmas shopping, and reading nine books for the literature course I had unthinkingly agreed to teach in the spring, my life was momentarily clear of the usual distractions. What do I mean by the usual distractions? My aged parents, my children, my former wives, my students, the Knicks, international crises, local crime (I recently had a car stolen), dreams of love.

    I was raring to go except for one minor though critical element. I was uninspired, had no ideas, merely will and desire and the grace of unexpected time. The blank screen in front of me pleaded for attention. I ventured an opening sentence, not a real one necessarily, more a claiming of territory. —The poet B left his house one morning in jacket and tie, shaved and showered, beard brushed, hair combed, at the top of his game, with the sense that he would never return. I studied the sentence a moment with burgeoning disappointment. Where could such a story go. I then effaced it word by word, leaving the initial 'B' so as not to have lost everything at once. The last thing I wanted was to find myself back at the beginning, that inhospitable, unnourishing, unfathomable place. That first violation of the page's blankness, no matter how minimal, made me feel I was on my way. I warned myself against unearned exhilaration.

It might be useful to have a subject, I thought, or an action, or an interesting attitude toward whatever material (though I had no material as yet). All I had was a character named B, the poet and fiction writer who represented me in my not yet fully conceived faux memoir. In virtually all of the chapters, some of which I thought of as stories in themselves, my stand-in, B, showed a sometimes amusing, often humiliating tendency to form obsessive attachments with inappropriate women. How many times could you go to that well without running dry? B's romantic pursuit of women who were, in some not easily defined way, bad news, was gradually, I imagined, losing its charm.

Well, I thought, who said that all fictional memoirs had to be charming? Involving might be sufficient, or affecting, or educational, or troubling, or inspiring, or violating. And even at his worst, and when was he otherwise, you couldn't say that B was totally charmless. There was something winning about his feckless passions. All he wanted was human contact and love and some small degree of happiness and as he was getting older he pursued these ordinary goals with a doomed-to-fail urgency. Impatience was his undoing, had always been—B had a childish, volatile nature. Well, yes, but he tended to hide his childish longings except from people who were close to him for extended periods of time. He passed in the eyes of the world—didn't he?—as an adult. It was a difficult disguise to pull off, but he managed it almost as well as most.

Since he never quite understood how the world worked, the most negligible of chores were an adventure for him. Air travel, which he suffered for the sake of his career (you couldn't give readings unless you were willing to fly), was invariably for B a wrenching transaction with the demons of the unknown. Most air passengers concerned themselves with take off and landing. B felt endangered any time he was off the ground. Not so anyone noticed of course, or not so he noticed anyone noticing. In the disguise of being an adult, B toughed out the ordinary. He thought superstitiously that if he worried enough about a potential disaster, he might escape unscathed. The worrying would assuage the gods of disaster perhaps. Or since it was the nature of disaster to happen unexpectedly, to worry about unhappy consequences was an almost sure way of avoiding them.

Since B was an exaggerated version of the author, I knew more about B than I knew what to do with, which was my problem at the moment as I faced the almost blank screen of my computer. I was ready to set B in motion—that was the point wasn't it?—but where, in what context? What could B do this time around that he hadn't already done?

I threw to the wind another chancy opening sentence. –It was not what B expected or imagined, not even one of the featured attractions of his idle hopes, which is what he said after the fact to anyone who would listen in defense of his behavior.

That was a little better than the first one, but still it opened into nothing or worse, into anything or everything. I had no idea at this point what B had done or where I intended to send him. B could be going to a sporting event, where he was to tie up with one of his sons. That might be an interesting possibility, a basketball game or baseball game, the tickets given to him by his publisher, say. The story dealing with the son's ambivalent feelings toward B which would reveal themselves through the dynamic of the game they were watching.

—

B could be waiting on a corner just down the street from Madison Square Garden for his son to arrive, this would be the first son of his third marriage. The son is already ten minutes late. B is wearing a gray, hooded full length down coat, an Italian coat purchased on sale at a now defunct Soho shop called Mano à Mano. His coat of course is of no importance to the story.

B is almost always on time, hates to wait, hates it when others are late. His son, the one he is waiting to meet, tends to be late for their appointments, is always armed with an almost acceptable excuse when he arrives.

One of the reasons B hates to wait is that he hates to waste time, hates to do nothing which is how it suits him to perceive waiting. So he walks up and back, walking a positive activity in his view, even if his pacing about is just a more energized version of staying in the same place. Occasionally, he glances at his watch to note his son's duration of lateness.

He wonders if his son is late with everyone or just with him. They have never talked much about it, his son an admirable person in almost all other ways, and B has gone out of his way not to make an issue of it. It concerns him that his son's lateness has to do with an unexpressed anger toward him. It has shown itself in other ways too, in off the cuff remarks his son has made, in things his son has written. B has dealt with it by looking the other way.

B muses on his own anger toward his own father—that's never gone away—and it strikes him that his son is behaving toward him as he's behaved toward his father. B has been a good father, he believes, but he has set a bad example as a son. It's not that B wants to be angry with his father—he's tried in his way to give it up—it's just that it's not in him not to be. He loves his father, but can hardly stand to be in the same room with him. B's son loves him, but is sometimes grudging about spending time with him, is chronically late for their appointments.

That his son is late (and getting later) gives B time to muse on this disappointing aspect of their relationship. At that moment, he notices a figure much like his son walking in his direction from some not easily determined distance, coming toward him while seeming—one of those odd city illusions—farther and farther away. He raises his arm to wave or thinks of raising it, not yet sure that the approaching figure is definitely his son. He experiences briefly (in a subliminal flash) the disappointment of thwarted expectation.

Is this really the story I wanted to tell when I knocked out my intentionally vague opening sentence?

The approaching figure in the distance is not his son, not even someone who much resembles him and B glances at his watch again, taking cognizance of fleeting time. His life is rushing by.

B, angry at being kept in suspension, feels a hand on his shoulder. –Dad, sorry, the son says. They embrace.

Or: his daughter arrives in his son's place, explaining that the son had to do something else, an unavoidable commitment, at the last minute.

Or: a young woman he doesn't know, has never seen before, has never heard his son mention, arrives, bearing his son's regrets. —Would you like to use his ticket? B asks.

—I can't she says. I have a prior commitment.

Or: a former wife, the mother of the son, arrives with a message from the son who blah blah blah, the wife willing, if he doesn't mind, to join him at the game. He does mind but is too polite or too cowardly or too much the gentleman to say so.

Or: A woman, a stranger, comes over to him and asks him (his son a half hour late) if he has an extra ticket to sell. He says he is waiting for someone but if that someone doesn't arrive in the next…20 minutes, she is welcome to the ticket. Twenty minutes is a long time to stand around on a snowy December night and the woman says she'll give twice the face value of the ticket. —Money is not the issue, B says. I'm waiting for my son. The notion outrages her and she gives B a skeptical look before straggling away.

There is no story unless the son arrives, at least not the story about father and son he had assigned himself to tell.

What's happened to the son, what's holding him up? Has the train broken down? Has he fallen asleep after staying up all night? Has he forgotten that this is the night of the game? Or maybe the son has forgotten that they arranged to meet at six o'clock in order to have dinner together and is planning to show up a few minutes before game time.

B starts to move into the Garden complex to find a phone when he feels a hand on his shoulder stopping his movement. —Hey, Dad, his son says, sorry. The trains were impossible.

So the story is back to its original premise. The son has shown up after all, hasn't forgotten the date, has only been, hardly a surprise given their recent history together, characteristically delayed.

—It's probably too late to find a restaurant, B says. We'll grab a bite inside.

On his way through the doors, his son ahead of him, B reaches into his coat pocket for the tickets and comes up empty. He distinctly remembers taking the ticket envelope out of his wallet and transferring it to his right-hand coat pocket. He tries the left side pocket, but it is no surprise not to find it there.

—Can't find the tickets, Dad? his son asks.

B admits to nothing, tries his pants pockets and then the interior breast pocket of his jacket.

He remembers when he was talking to the woman, the one who wanted to buy a ticket from him, reaching into his coat pocket and feeling the envelope. It strikes him that she may have had a confederate come up behind him while they were talking—she had stayed around chatting him up—and the confederate had taken the ticket envelope from his pocket. In fact, he remembers, or thinks he does, a slight brush from behind during his conversation with the woman.

Out of the side of his eye, he notices the woman standing with her back to one of the ticket-takers, a man next to her talking to someone else. He pulls at his son's arm and without a word of explanation hurries toward the woman. She notices him and smiles in a friendly, slightly mocking way.

—You've found your son, she says to him, and I've found my ticket.

Her friendliness puts B at a disadvantage and he is embarrassed to accuse her of what may be a wholly unfounded suspicion. —Where did you get your ticket? he asks as if a casual question.

—This nice man here, she says, pointing to the expensively dressed thug next to her, had an extra that he's graciously let me have. The son looks from the woman to his father to the thug and has an immediate take on the situation. —Don't Dad, he whispers to B. Meaning don't make a scene please. B is fuming, though conflicted. His son is like his former wife in that it embarrasses him to be associated with someone behaving badly in public.

B can't be sure of course, and feels he has no right to make accusations on circumstantial evidence, but his gut feeling (not always reliable in the past) advises him that these people have taken advantage of him, have stolen his tickets, have ripped him off, and what is he going to do about it?

—Nice to meet you, the woman says to his son as she and the thug go through the gate together, the man holding the tickets in such a way as to make it difficult for B to determine their color.

—What was that about? the son asks.

B shrugs. —What do you think it was about? he says.

The son laughs. —Is it multiple choice? he asks. You imagine, probably wrongly, that the woman you spoke to had something to do with your lost tickets. Is that close?

B shrugs, a partial acknowledgment.

He hates more than anything to be taken advantage of, or (which is the same and different) to feel he has been taken advantage of. His obsession is to call the editor who gave him the tickets, find out the seat numbers and have the thieves dragged from their ill-gotten seats. —What we could do, he says, is get a good dinner somewhere and pass up the game or go to a sports bar and have dinner, such as it might be, and watch the game while we stuff our faces.

—Well, I could just go home and watch the game on my own set, the son says with undisguised irritation. Dad, how could you have possibly lost the tickets?

—I didn't lose them, B says. They were stolen from my pocket.

—By those people you were talking to before?

B nods. —That's my best guess, he says.

—Dad, the son says, aggrieved with his father, you shouldn't have let them get away with it.

———

Scrolling the text backward, I reread what I have written, changing a phrase here and there, grumbling to myself at the paucity of the imagining. Then I turn off the screen, shutting out B and his son who are still (and will remain) standing around in the cavernous lobby of Madison Square Garden, in one of those temporary states of inertia and disappointment that have been known to last a lifetime.

2.

It is only when B goes into his wallet for his gold Visa Card to pay for their overpriced retro-gourmet dinner does he discover that the game tickets are in his billfold in the very place he stashed them earlier. How strange that he had looked everywhere else for the tickets but hadn't taken the trouble to check his wallet. So certain he had been that the tickets had been stolen. If they can find a taxi right away and the traffic isn't too bad, they can get back to the Garden in time to see most of the second half.

It takes a few harried minutes to find an unoccupied cab in the mood to stop for them. The son does not berate B for what must seem impossibly foolish to semi-crazy behavior on his father's part, but wears a muted ironic smile.

—I guess it's good that you didn't accuse those people of stealing your tickets, Dad, he says as soon as they reenter the Garden complex.

B lets his son's remark echo in his head and wonders whether to take umbrage although in all probability he already has.

They arrive at their seats almost five minutes into the third quarter with the Knicks behind by eleven points. Momentarily, Harper hits a three pointer and the deficit is cut to eight.

—Maybe we'll bring them luck, the son says. The two teams exchange wasted opportunities and B can see that his team is as flat as last week's opened club soda.

3.

The Knicks are only one point behind Portland going into the fourth quarter, but B has a sinking feeling about the outcome, a sense that his team's will is deficient tonight, which is what he says.

—Don't be so pessimistic, Dad, his son says. You always think the worst is going to happen.

It's true that he feels that way some of the time, perhaps much of the time, perhaps always in conjunction with sporting events in which he has a rooting interest. The thing is, he tends to be right in these dire intuitions more often than not, and what a pleasure it is when he happens to be wrong. The Knicks score the first basket of the fourth quarter on a breakaway layup by Starks off a steal by Oakley. B is encouraged, but doesn't allow himself to dare to hope.

—

I have not yet decided on the outcome of the game. Either alternative, win or lose, provides a banal or unsurprising resolution. What if the story cuts away to something else—to B and his son walking to the subway after the game—the instant the potentially winning shot left the shooter's hands. Unfair to the reader, of course, but more interesting than the more conventional alternatives.

The Knicks move up by five with seven minutes to go, more an example of attrition than exceptional play.

—You still think they're going to lose, Dad? his son asks.

Before he can answer, someone on Portland hits a three point shot and the lead is reduced to two.

—This game is up for grabs, B says. Whoever wants it more is going to win.

—Whoever's going to win is going to win, the son says with a smile. That's a paraphrase.

—No it isn't, B says. Portland and the Knicks exchange baskets and the lead remains at two with the Knicks in possession of the ball, moving tentatively down the floor. A familiar-looking woman sitting catty-cornered to B catches his eye and winks at him. He tries to remember where he knows her from and draws a blank. A moment later it strikes him that he had met her at a meeting of a 12-step group called Heartbreak Anonymous.

While the two teams move back and forth in sometimes capricious, sometimes desperate haste before his eyes, B finds himself musing on his impatient wait for his son earlier in the evening. The pavement is icy and he can feel the damp through the soles of the gray New Balance running shoes he wears for all occasions. He remembers walking up and back to keep the blood flowing, hands stuffed in his pockets, taking stock of the folks that precede him through the Garden doors. By being late, his son has in some sense reversed roles with him (B's father had been invariably late for their appointments particularly when he was small).

Suddenly he is aware that the people around him have risen to their feet and are clapping their hands and shouting encouragement. B glances at the scoreboard and notices that the Knicks are up by six with two minutes and 20 seconds left to play. His son, standing next to him, puts his arm around B's shoulders and gives him a proprietary hug. Portland misses a three-point attempt, but the Knicks eager for the rebound lose the ball out of bounds in an in-house dispute. B groans as if his own failed poise were responsible for the error.

B remembers the time he played the game in college, a back-up point guard on a team that lost almost twice as many games as they won. There was this one game in particular he remembers when he got a chance to start against a local rival (the usual starter having come down with food poisoning or some such thing) and he had the game of his life. He had missed his first two shots embarrassingly and had decided to focus his attention on the passing game. The first shot he made was in the waning seconds of the first half, a buzzer beater from considerably beyond his range. He had made the shot after taking the ball away from someone who was trying to dribble around him. Encouraged by his teammates' praise, he found himself "in the zone" in the second half, the ball doing whatever he asked of it. He made passes he had seen great point guards make on television, hit shots he had never even attempted in practices. With each success, he grew more daring and inspired. It was as if he had become someone else.

After his brilliant game, his basketball career was all mediocrity and dissatisfaction, the magic returning only for the briefest of moments to remind him what he had once done and would likely never do again. His own shadow achievement taunted him. He held himself to a standard that had been achieved through accidental grace so he suffered continued and renewed disappointment.

The Knicks have two foul shots coming and a two point lead with 43 seconds left to play. Starks is at the line, a good foul shooter with a history of making the clutch basket, a man with metaphoric ice water in his veins. So why does B have this doomed and sinking feeling? Starks makes the first foul shot, the first the more difficult of the two. The applause is thunderous. Half the sellout crowd is on its feet. Starks takes a deep breath before taking the second, cannot be accused of not giving the shot his undivided attention. Nevertheless it rims the basket and comes out, Portland grabbing the rebound and calling time.

—Good game, huh? B says to his son.

—Not so much good as close, the son says, but maybe that's what you mean.

The Knicks commit themselves to preventing a three-point shot, but Portland has a different tactic in mind. Strickland fakes the perimeter shot then drives to the basket and makes an uncontested lay-up, reducing the lead to one point. As soon as the Knicks inbound the ball, Mason is fouled. This doesn't seem a wise move in B's unprofessional estimate since there are still 27 seconds left in the game. Mason misses the first foul shot, makes the second.

—Nervous time, his son says to him.

B wants to tell him it will be all right, not to worry, but he can find no words of comfort to offer. He squeezes his son's arm in commiseration. He himself is full of hope but distrusts it all.

The crowd, much of it, most of it, gets to its feet and roars in one ear-shattering voice, —Dee-fense. Dee-fense. B wonders why, even among people who share his aims, he feels himself an outsider.

The same Knick defense, the same Portland play, but this time Strickland is fouled driving to the basket and if the game is to be tied he will have to do it from the foul line. He makes one out of two, and the Knicks rebound again and are fouled again. There are now 11 seconds of nail biting tedium left. B looks up at the electronic scoreboard to confirm that the Knicks are winning 91 to 90.

The standing crowd hushes as Harper gets ready to take his first foul shot. He misses short and as soon as the ball clunks against the front of the rim, the crowd lets out a collective groan.

—They don't want to win, B says in the voice of self-protective disappointment.

—Well, they do and they don't, his son says.

Harper makes the second, extending the lead to two. While Portland takes a timeout to design the shot that will either win the game for them or force a tie, B feels a tightness in his chest. Why does he take this all so personally? The answer is: he just does. It is his childish nature to identify with his team. As Portland gets ready to make the inbounds pass, B is aware, frighteningly so, of how much is at stake for him. More than that, his team doesn't deserve to win.

With five seconds left, Strickland goes around a pick and drives toward the basket. Several Knick players converge to cut him off. Rather than force his shot, the Portland guard whips the ball out into the right corner where Majerle waits in readiness behind the three point line. The uncontested shot is launched like a dagger to B's heart. Watching out of the corner of his eye as if anticipating some kind of unacceptable cinematic violence, he concedes the game. He sees the ball arc toward the basket—where else can it go?—intruding into the sacred space of the net. He withholds his dissatisfaction, takes his defeat like a martyr. The shot, though in perfect trajectory, falls short, hitting nothing but the outstretched hands of several players. Someone, some hand, thrusts the ball up into the basket but it doesn't matter, the game is already recorded history. The clock has run out, the sound of the buzzer overwhelmed by the screaming of the crowd. It is another disappointment, Portland's loss, his team having won despite itself.

B and his son move in single file through the corridors toward the exit, the crowd impinging on them, pulling them apart. In fact, when he steps out into the frigid night air, B finds himself alone, his son who had been a step or two behind him nowhere to be seen. There are a number of exits and perhaps when they had gotten separated, his son had veered off accidentally in another direction. B steps back inside, parting the crowd, and forces his way fretfully back into the arena where he has already experienced both victory and loss.

—

All of the above takes place in B's mind as he paces back and forth outside the Garden in the soft inconsequential snow. The game has not been played, not yet, is 20 minutes short of opening tip, though B has already concocted a scenario for its outcome. His son, who is late, who he loves better than himself, who he believes he sees in the distance hurrying toward him, has not quite reached him, will not

B

reach him for another instant or so, though he is already imagining the son's casually presented excuse for his lateness, and in response his own gracious anger-denied acceptance, as the son continues indefinitely, in some waking dream that B is always just about to escape, to make his long-awaited, imperceptible approach.

V. THE BLIND DATE

B, lonely and horny in no notable order of priority, takes out an ad in the Personals Section of *New York* magazine. "Divorced Writer, heavy drinker and sports enthusiast, seeks attractive, intelligent, generous woman between 35 and 49. Sensualist preferred. Object whatever." Three days after the ad appears, expecting zilch for his troubles, he receives a packet with seventy-seven answers. He is capable of dealing with five or even ten responses, but seventy-seven is an unwieldy mob. He is reminded of the sequence in the Buster Keaton movie, "Seven Chances," in which, having advertised for a bride, Buster wakes from a nap at the church to discover hordes of furious women determined to marry him.

B files the 77 responses away under "Blind Date," two weeks passing before he is up to sorting through the perfumed lies. What he does in the cause of efficiency, some platonic ideal of, is to break down the responses into three basic categories—Hopeless, Possible, Bull's-eye. On a cursory reading of the letters, he finds himself with nine Hopeless and 68 Possibles, a problematic grouping. Among the Possibles, he wants to believe, there will be a Bull's-eye in the rough. It is not so much that B knows what he wants as that he is confident that what he wants will make itself known when the right woman presents herself. Another week passes before he calls the first five of the more engaging Possibles—he has broken them down into More Possible and Less—arranging to meet for drinks with two of the More Possible women he has interviewed on the phone. Without thinking the logistics through, he schedules the appointments forty-five minutes apart. What the hell is he doing? he wonders briefly. The doing itself, the compulsive process, has taken over.

The time comes to meet the first of his two appointments—MP1, as he thinks of her—and B finds himself excessively eager, so eager that compensatory inertia overtakes him and he is unable to leave home for the longest time. So he arrives at the Brass Bar, the place of assignation, a favorite watering hole of his, significantly late. This is not, he knows, God knows, the way to make a favorable impression. Anyway, he is disappointed on sight, assuming (red dress, reddish hair) that she is who she is, the one (the first) he has made blind arrangements to meet. If so, she isn't what he has in mind, her letter (unless he has confused it with another) suggesting a different assortment of attributes.

How to explain this immediate nonnegotiable disappointment. It is not that the woman is not attractive (he has anticipated his respondents overrating their attractiveness), but that she is too conventionally pretty, not the kind of person who would need to answer a Personals ad to find a man. He is not prepared to deal with a near-beauty. In panic, he leaves the restaurant and walks around the block, looking for a place to have a drink. When he returns to the Brass Bar, prepared to explain himself—he means to be up front about his evasive behavior—she is gone. It is almost time for the second of his two appointments and he sits down in the booth that the redheaded woman, who may or may not be MP1, has vacated. B takes off his jacket, straightens his tie (while opening the top button of his shirt), brushes his hand through his hair. Waiting for nothing, he advises himself against excessive expectation.

His second appointment is not coming, he decides with a barely perceptible sigh of relief, looking the other way when a small dark woman occupies the bench across from him. There's something grim about her, though she offers him, or seems to, a minimal smile. He says, –Hi, and holds out his hand. She is writing something on a napkin in a small cramped hand, which she pushes across the table to him. –Hi to you, the message says. It is signed, Gloria M.

B

B accepts the terms of her communication (assuming what?), asks her in writing on the back of the same napkin if she would like a glass of wine.

She studies his text, a quizzical look on her face, then nods. The waiter appears just as B is about to signal to him, and he orders two glasses of wine, one white, one red, covering both bases, glancing at his silent date out of the corner of his eye. She is almost pretty, her face a bit pinched. He is trying to remember what she said about herself in her letter. It's not likely that she's "Beautiful, widowed concert flutist, mother of five," or "Single, Jewish, perky Tarot reader and channeler with a passionate love of life." Perhaps "Divorced poet, broodingly sexual, with five year-old daughter," or "Active and involved academic, 42, well-endowed with looks, brains and wry humor." None of his correspondents had advertised herself as mute or with a predilection to silence.

When the wine comes, he offers her her choice of red or white, putting both glasses in front of her. What she does is take a drink of the white, then refill the glass with the red, stirring the mix with a finger. –What's the point of that? B asks, to which she seems almost to smile.

Before he can claim the remains of the red, Gloria M has poured some of the mix into that glass, creating two glasses of hybrid. She slides both glasses in his direction and mouths the words, –You choose.

When he takes the glass that has not touched her lips, she turns her face away in apparent disappointment. He quickly recognizes his mistake, so he takes a sip of the near-red and moves to exchange glasses with her. She slaps his hand away before he can complete the transaction. Another humbling surprise.

B considers leaving, but something inexplicable holds him to the spot. Fascination perhaps or the inexplicable stirrings of his ungoverned self. He sulks. Gloria writes something on her napkin and then, rereading what she has written, blacks it out.

–What have you decided not to tell me? B asks her.

Her expression mocks him or seems to. Her mouth forms the word, "What?" She pushes the blacked-out message across the table to him. The longer he stares at the effaced message, which runs three full lines and a part of a fourth, the more he senses the gist of the hidden text. He sees or imagines he sees the words "loneliness" and "desire." He reaches over and takes her hand, which she filigrees into his. He imagines the table between them lifting into the air, torn from its moorings by the wistful aspirations of desire.

When their hands come apart, she scratches a message on his palm with a finger. At this moment, the woman, who had been at the table earlier, the near beautiful redhead, reenters the restaurant.

B catches her image in the bar mirror and instinctively ducks his head as if he felt the need to hide from her. When he looks up, she is standing at the table staring at him. —Don't I know you? she says to him.

Her question seems to pin him to the wall. —I'm sometimes mistaken for a famous trial lawyer, B says.

—I know what you mean, she says, but that's not who I was thinking of.

—If we had met, B says, it isn't likely I would have forgotten you. He turns his attention to Gloria, who is twirling her empty wine glass, offers her the consolation of a shrug.

The redheaded woman, whom he imagines to be the "perky Tarot reader," persists. —Aren't you 'divorced writer and sports enthusiast,' blah blah blah, she says.

He reluctantly admits to being that very person, though can't imagine how she knows.

Gloria takes B's napkin and writes furiously on it, then she gets up, hands the napkin to the other woman, and leaves the booth. She has, he notices for the first time, a barely perceptible limp.

After the redheaded woman reads Gloria's note, she says —No thank you, to no one in particular and turns to go.

In a moment, both women have left the restaurant. He has, as he sees it, in one try failed twice. Inertia and a sense of responsibility toward the bill keeps B from immediately rushing after the women, Gloria M in particular, his imagination on short leash. Collecting himself, slipping on his suede jacket, he notices a dark brown leather pouch on Gloria's side of the booth.

She'll discover its absence, he tells himself, so he sits down again, orders a double Scotch with a Rolling Rock on the side, and awaits her anticipated return, rehearsing to himself some of the things he wants to say to her. —You're the one I was looking for when I took the ad, he imagines himself saying. Even in the sanctity of the imagination, B's amorous claim loses conviction the moment it is given voice.

When an hour passes without her reappearance, he looks in the purse for identification, the name Cassandra Lutz written on a license and two credit cards. There is no address anywhere. There is also a hairbrush, a paperback of The Scarlet Letter and a wallet containing three dollars. B stuffs the soft leather pouch in his jacket pocket, pays the bill and exits the Brass Bar.

In a fever of desolation, he wanders, head down, in the direction of his small apartment on First Street and Avenue A. It begins to rain in a desultory way and he puts up the collar of his coat. He is about to duck into a ratso bar to dry off—he could do with another drink—when someone grabs his arm. It is the redheaded woman (the appointment he didn't keep), her face wet, rain coursing down her cheeks. —I've been trying to catch up to you, she says. You have my purse, I believe. She retrieves it from his pocket, going through the contents with an accountant's eye in a way that suggests distrust.

Now that she is standing next to him, B notices that she has a nasty scar on her face on the side she tends to keep turned away. The flaw in her beauty makes her seem less resistible and he invites her to have a drink with him.

—I don't drink, she says. I used to, but I don't now, okay? Besides you don't want to go into that place—believe me, you don't.

He can see nothing wrong with the place besides it being rundown and ugly.

They stand under the eaves of the ratso bar, the rain encroaching on the protruding tips of their shoes, while they sort out logistics. The woman has something unpleasant to tell him and B has agreed to hear her out. The question is where can they go to have this one-sided conversation. The longer they hang out in the rain, his feet beginning to soak, the more B craves a drink. It is Gloria M he perceives himself to want, the lost, unforgiving, and mysteriously silent Gloria.

When the mild rain slows to a heavy mist, the scarred redheaded woman suggests they walk around the block.

—Just who do you think you are? she says sotto voce.

—What? It is always the same question.

—Your thoughtless behavior, as you must know, has generated mucho anger in certain circles, she says, taking his arm. —I just wanted to warn you, that's all. Nothing at all may come of it, but it's always well to be prepared. A word to the wise, that kind of thing.

Her insinuation troubles B, irritates him no end. What thoughtless behavior? What does she think he's done?

—That you don't have a clue is in some ways a worse offense than the other, she says in answer to his consternation. That's the nature so to speak of the beast. Innocence is not an excuse any more. Let me add that I'm not one of those who has gotten her hackles up. I probably would have done exactly the same thing in your place. You never know, do you?

B, feeling anything but thankful, thanks her for her concern, says he has to go, inventing various urgencies to justify an immediate departure.

She holds onto his arm as they slosh along in the downpour and he remembers that one of his correspondents was a sucker for "long romantic walks in the rain."

—Do you want to come to my place? he asks.

—There's no quit in you, is there? she says, handing him a business card: Cassandra L—Astrologist, Channeler, Reader of Signs. —If you need me, I'm at this number for you.

When he gets home, B finds the door to his apartment ajar and Cassandra's warning comes back to him with a rush. He remembers double locking the door when he left, or thinks he remembers. Someone has gotten into his apartment and may still be there, waiting for him with harmful intent. What should B do? He rings the bell of his neighbor's apartment and hears the dog bark, a plaintive call. He has heard the animal's sorrowful cry any number of times, but he has never actually seen it.

B hits the streets, looking for a cop or a weapon, someone or something to accompany him in his confrontation with the unknown. Ten minutes later, B returns alone (a rock in each pocket) and enters his place with clattering stealth, heart in an uproar.

A grizzled older man he has never seen before, sitting in the velvet arm chair in his living room, introduces himself in a mild voice as an aggrieved father. The man's mildness temporarily assuages B's sputtering outrage.

—How did you get in here? he asks. No friend to the inordinate security apparently necessary to living in New York City, B nevertheless has always taken the requisite precautions.

—I've come to you to ask you to stay away from my daughter, the man says. If you have even a shred of decency, which is your reputation among my sources, you'll do as I ask.

—I hardly know your daughter, B says. Anyway, which one is your daughter?

—Just give me your word that you'll stay away from her, and there'll be no recriminations. I have a disgraceful temper, but I have always considered myself a fair man.

—Whatever you say, B says, eager to have his apartment to himself, though as soon as he's offered his accord, he feels repelled by his own cowardice. —I mean, in all likelihood, you have nothing to worry about from me.

—I'm just asking this one thing, the man says, looking up at him with blind eyes. —One thing is all I'm asking of you. He points his cane in B's direction. You won't grant me that one thing? The intruder lumbers to his feet and taps his way to the door. —A curse on your head, he says, an eerie smile on his thick lips as he works his way out of the apartment.

Fifteen minutes later, B gets a silent phone call. B conjectures that the father has told the daughter (Gloria M?) that he won't be dissuaded by threats from his determination to see her. His stance, he imagines, has encouraged her to call. He says, —Hello, twice, his enthusiasm compounding itself, while imagining in the inescapable silence her unspoken message. —I'm glad you called, he says to the void. Then B suggests meeting her for breakfast the next morning at a hippie pancake place called Tofu Forever. Before he can suggest a time—he is thinking of suggesting 11—his silent caller hangs up the phone.

At this point, he notices the flickering red light on his answering machine and he pushes the playback button to check out his messages. There is only one and it is from a woman apologizing for not keeping her appointment with him at the Brass Bar. A case of cold feet, she says. Also, her former live-in boy friend had returned.

If the one who left the message was the one he was supposed to meet, then who, B asks himself, is Gloria M? Given his infatuation with her, B may have willfully evaded the obvious. Clearly, she is not any of the women he talked to on the phone and certainly not either of the two he had arranged to meet. Their meeting, it is clear to him now, was some kind of fortuitous misunderstanding. B, whose loneliness and horniness remain unabated, feels temporarily blessed. So, undaunted, even spurred by the father's warning, he goes to Tofu Forever to keep the appointment he had made (or had not made) with his silent caller. After three coffees, nursed and untasted, and a concomitant passage of time, he resigns himself grudgingly to another situation of terminal misunderstanding. A weight of loss, chronic since childhood, revisits with renewed intensity. When he gets up to leave, he discovers an even stronger disposition not to move and so he sits down again. Another half hour passes with characteristic haste. He daydreams, remembers the last time he was in love and the last time he fell out of love. It seems like a hundred years ago and also like yesterday.

A sense that someone is staring at him brings him back from the world of fleeting memory to the unchanging moment. When he looks up what he notices is the nervy Cassandra staring at him through the glass in the front door. There seem to be six or seven women standing alongside or behind her. One, though it is probably a trick of the light, seems to be shaking her fist at him.

A white-haired man, apparently the owner of Tofu Forever, comes over to his table, says he doesn't want any trouble in his place. —Why should there be any trouble? B asks.

—You know, the man says, making the slightest gesture with his head toward the door. The group of women standing behind Cassandra seems to have tripled in number in the intervening five minutes between glances in that direction.

—It's all a misunderstanding, B says. Nevertheless, he follows the white-haired man into the employees bathroom behind the kitchen and climbs through an open window into a courtyard.

—Be careful, the owner calls after him. That's a mean-looking crowd.

Not sure which way to go, he climbs a fence into the adjacent yard, exciting some fearsome barks from an unseen dog. He goes from backyard to backyard, shimmying up and down fences, trying to outflank the crowd of women. He falls only once, tearing his pants in a minor way. The last backyard leads to a narrow alleyway, which he follows to a street apparently around the corner from the entrance to the restaurant. He looks both ways before emerging. His sense of direction askew—even in the best of circumstances it was never wholly reliable—B starts in one direction then changes his mind and goes off in the other. He has only to peer around the corner to see that it is the right choice he has forsaken for the wrong one. So he turns around again and runs two blocks without looking back. Out of breath, he takes his chances and veers into a bar that has a similar under lit dark-wood ambience to the Brass Bar. This place could be its clone.

Out of perhaps unnecessary precaution, he takes the farthest vacant booth from the door and is about to take a seat when he notices a familiar figure seated, her hand in front of her face, across the aisle from him. She doesn't look up when he slides into the booth facing her. B starts to say the same thing several times, an acknowledgment of his pleasure in finding her again.

At some point, she slips her hand across the table into his, only to reclaim it the moment he catches her eye. An uncharacteristic shyness ties his tongue in knots. Stammering the request like some backward teenager, he asks her for her phone number.

She writes on her napkin, holding it up to him: —I have no phone. What for?

—You need a phone so I can get in touch with you, he writes on his own napkin and passes it to her.

When she smiles at him—her smile a rare event—B tells her a few of the things he's imagined himself saying. This is out of character for him. It is not B's habit to announce his feelings directly. The thought, for B, the felt unspoken, has always for better or worse sufficed. The news of his interest in her (his passion, his affection) seems to disturb rather than delight. She seems to shut down, withdraws more deeply into herself. The more she retreats from him into the abyss of self, the more impelled B is to make contact. The way he does it is to tell her who he is, which he does by retailing anecdotes about his life that do him no credit. He wants her to see that his fallibility matches hers.

For starters, he tells her about the breakup of his first marriage, stuff he has never told anyone before. How, just months after his first child was born, he had walked out on his wife. Well, not exactly walked out—he had told her he was leaving, feeling it the honorable thing to do—but then he had left the state (they had been living in California) without leaving a forwarding address. He sent money for the first year, monthly sums, whatever he could afford. But then she moved and neglected to send him the address and his checks came back like boomerangs through no fault of his own. He had been very young, too young to know what to do with a child, the pregnancy an apparent accident, though his suspicions had been that she had deceived him by not putting in her diaphragm after telling him she had.

Even so, his behavior was regrettable. He acknowledges that now. His urgent need to get away a kind of madness or childishness. Now, years later, he sometimes wakes in the middle of the night aware of having lost a child he may never find.

And that wasn't the worst of his mistakes with women, only the most unforgivable. His third marriage broke up because he discovered his wife was having an affair (with her therapist of all people) and he couldn't forgive her, wouldn't. Not that she ever asked to be forgiven, not that she even stopped the affair even after he confronted her with what he knew.

After a few minutes, Gloria gets up, indicates through gesture (a single tear leaning from her eye) that she has to leave.

–How will I find you again? he asks.

Her answer is to hurry away, her long coat trailing like a shadow along the ground. She flees, he follows. He wants, needs, to see where she goes. To keep her continually in sight is security against never seeing her again. After a few blocks of this regimen, she turns around and returns to him, assaulting him with a hard push in the chest, sending him backward into the unexplored landscape of surprise.

Stumbling backwards, B chooses not to fall. The moment his equilibrium has been reestablished, he holds out his hand to his assailant. Gloria M slaps at it violently and misses, B impulsively pulling back, an unthinking gesture he immediately regrets. Hit me if that's what you want, he wants to say but censors.

Gloria stands facing him with inchoate fury, her face red. He tells her that he loves her as if that alone were missing from their dialogue. Unable to find her memo pad, she writes on his cuff, –I never want to see you again. Can't you understand that? In his time, he has understood more difficult things than that; he has seen through the opaque, has read between the lines, has made intuitive sense of unparaphrasable language. The unknown has often lingered like sadness at his fingertips.

B rereads the note on his cuff, straining for another way of making sense of its text. This isn't the first time he's been rejected. But it always seems like the first time, doesn't it? As he walks away, he consoles himself with the notion that her unqualified rejection of him is only words on his cuff. When he gets home, his neighbor, a woman of uncertain age—the one with the plaintive dog—intercepts him in front of his apartment and tells him that just a few minutes ago, a small army of women were waiting in the narrow hallway for him. –You just missed them. I hope it wasn't anything too important.

–You know how it is, B says, you innocently throw a stone in a well and the reverberations go on for the rest of your life.

–Is that a fact? the neighbor says, rolling her eyes, slipping into her apartment and closing the door.

In an undoing mood, B puts all the letters he got in response to his ad in the waste basket and burns them. It takes awhile and the residual smoke hangs on afterwards, plaguing him. The smell of smokey perfume, with a charred subtext, lingers. In the bathroom, with the window open, B, looking for something to read, entertains the text on his cuff. The thing is, it has faded (or it was the left cuff and not, as he remembered, the right) and he checks the other cuff and then the other. Gloria M's rejection note has vanished. Is that a positive sign, he wonders, or an indication of a different problem altogether?

He writes a poem, or the beginning of one, called "Undoing the Past." His thesis is, that contrary to the received view, not only can the past be undone, it is undone, despite the usual desperate attempts to hold on to it like a secret truth, all the time.

In a short month, he has fully recovered from Gloria's loss and is back at his job teaching creative writing at one of the branches of the City University. He has stopped drinking temporarily, has even gone to an AA Meeting, though more out of curiosity than acknowledgment, sitting like an eavesdropper in the back row. An unexpected contentment holds him in its grasp.

One day he writes a story about a writer like himself, thrice divorced, lonely and horny (sometimes horny and lonely) who takes an ad out in a Personals column of a local magazine. In the story, the writer meets an apparent blind woman (he is never wholly sure she is blind) to whom he is unaccountably drawn. He pursues her recklessly and loses her. She distrusts his ardor, is unable to believe anyone would want her the way he professes to want her. At the end of the story, months after he has given up on her, there is a knock on his door in the middle of the night. He knows even before he answers the door that it is the blind woman and that she has decided to accept him but that—the passage of time perhaps responsible—he has only the dimmest recollection of his once all-consuming passion for her.

Even as he opens the door, even before he sees her, he makes a decision as to how to proceed. He will pretend that everything is as it was, that he still loves her to distraction. It is, as he sees it, the only honorable choice allowed him. He faces her, as the story ends, with words of endearment on his tongue and disappointment—the sadness of irrecoverable loss—on his unseen face.

VI. LOST IN EROS

1.
It was not what B expected or imagined, not even one of the featured attractions of his idle hopes, which is what he said after the fact to anyone who would listen in defense of his behavior. He was not one of these older men who out of denial and God knows what else pursued much younger women. That had never been his game. He had simply, without premeditation, during a reading in Seattle, found himself turned inside out by someone—a woman, a girl really—who happened to be thirty plus years his junior.

This girl had come up to him after his reading, carrying three of his books, asking if....The story doesn't bear repeating. Asking if he wouldn't mind—her shyness was exquisite—if it wasn't too much trouble....The completed sentence was a tacit collaboration between them. –You want me to sign your books, is that it? he asked. I'd be honored.

–They're your books, she said. I'm just their reader.

She opened the top one—*A Fictional Autobiography*—to the title page, and handed him a pen. He asked her her name, which seemed to fluster her. –I just want to know how to inscribe it, he added, embarrassed by her embarrassment.

–It doesn't matter, she said, then mumbled her name, turning her face away. It sounded to him as if she were introducing herself as 'anyone'. She was not beautiful, perhaps almost beautiful, her face too narrow, her features wayward as if at some point they had taken a misguided turn. Her eyes were an astonishing shade of green.

He poised the pen over the page, waiting for further instructions.

She had straight pitch-black hair, which she wore down her narrow back like a waterfall. She was neither tall nor short. Her gestures had an unaffected elegance. He signed the books with willed deliberation, hoarding his time with her. It was unavailing. In a moment, she was gone, leaving his life irrecoverably, walking away like a diminishing shadow toward the door.

He did what any infatuated 54-year-old author on a book signing tour might do; he left his post and followed her out the door.

When he caught up with her she seemed unsurprised at his presence. —Are you off on some urgent call? he asked. Something life and death?

She shrugged, wrinkled her brow in exhaustive thought. —Why don't you join us for drinks after the signing, he said. I promise I'll be quick. I'll use both hands and sign two books at a time.

—Is quickness such a virtue? she asked, chewing on her lip. She took his hand, fetched it from his side, and swung it carelessly between them. —I don't really drink.

When he told me about it, that spontaneous gesture, the swinging of his hand in her odd girlish way, he said it was like the sealing of some terrible bargain between them. He took one long hopeless longing look back, waving his head in desperate negation like a fighter quitting a bout because he no longer had the heart for unrelieved punishment.

He went back with her to her place, which she shared, as it turned out, with a bearded man (with a small pony tail) about her own age. Penelope, which was the name she had obliquely refused to give him, introduced him to the guy in residence. She called him PT.

B was gracious though disappointed, while PT registered surly indifference. The place was small and skanky with a soupcon of extremely marginal charm. Two plants, some posters, a drawing of Penelope, some Chianti bottles with candles in them. Tempted to leave, B wanted to get some kind of take first on this other relationship. Perhaps they weren't lovers, perhaps it was something else, an arrangement peculiar to people of that age in this time. He invented two or three almost acceptable scenarios.

When B left, babbling some incoherent excuse about having to get back to his hotel by a certain time, Penny caught up with him before he reached the next corner.

–I don't want you to take away the wrong impression, she said. PT and I are just going through the motions.

What motions were those? he wondered. –Of course it's none of my business, B said, which made her almost smile, a minor flaw in an unrelenting sadness. –I appreciate your telling me this anyway. B was not ready to confess his infatuation.

Penny looked over her shoulder, shrugged. –You're not jealous of PT, are you? Please! Don't disappoint me. She shuffled her feet, her bright face full of unacknowledged language.

A sudden unreasoning impulse overtook B. –Come with me, he said.

He saw that she was tempted. –Come with you where? she asked, amused and skeptical.

New York, B thought, but that wasn't what he had in mind when he blurted out his feckless invitation. –How old are you anyway? he said.

–I'm 20…well I'll be 20 in less than a month, she said. Look, I don't know what you want. If you want to be around me, is that what this is about, you could just hang out in Seattle for awhile, couldn't you? The possibility held him in its grasp for five prolonged minutes.

B flew back to New York that night on his scheduled flight and was met at Kennedy by a former wife who had maintained a longstanding officious interest in the vagaries of his life. It was a mistake, he knew, to confide the inexplicable attachment that occupied him like a demon, so he avoided talking about Penelope through the appetizer course of their dinner at Orso's. B was not a man to keep secrets forever, his heart a readily available, much-read book.

While waiting for the main course, he mentioned his inappropriate attachment, making as little of it as tiresome obsession allowed.

The former wife, raising her eyebrows and smiling broadly, said, —Wouldn't it be simpler to just put a "kick me" sign on your back?

When they lived together, it was she who had been the advocate of unreasoning impulse, B on the other side wherever that might be.

B's correspondence with Penelope went on for almost four months before he found an occasion, more excuse than occasion, to visit Seattle again.

Seeking the element of surprise, he arrived at Penelope's doorstep, bearing like a torch a bouquet of wilted anemones. When it became apparent that no one was home, he recognized the face of a fool in his own self-regarding mirror.

He waited, slumped down in his rental car, for her return. Two hours passed. It might have been a month. It had the texture of a lifetime. Then she arrived, getting out of a late model green Mercury, an older man (a man around B's age) at the wheel. She sauntered to the door of her small house, put a key in the lock and then withdrew it, turning as if she felt B's eyes on the back of her head.

He watched her approach his rental car, her route somewhat circuitous. She stared through the window at him for a moment or so, squinting her eyes against the glare, before running toward the passenger side of the car. —What a great surprise, she said, getting in, sliding her arms around his neck. I thought when I saw the parked car that you were the creep that had been making the sick phone calls.

—No such luck, he said.

They drove around looking for a secluded place to stop the car.

B

—Is PT still churl in residence? he willed himself to ask. He was like a college student around her, his unsureness poking through a smoke screen of bravado.

—I've told PT he has to leave, she said, signalling with a charming heavenward glance the impossibility of the man. He says he'll go when he finds another place. He doesn't even pay his share of the rent.

She had her arm around his shoulder while he drove. Even outside the city limits, absolute privacy seemed a rare commodity.

He told those in his circle—it was the same lie he told himself—that it wasn't sex or not primarily sex behind his feelings for the girl. He would be content, he insisted, just to take her to dinner or walk with her in the park. That was before she went down on him in the back seat of his rented Dodge Polaris. The earth moved or his emergency brake slipped.

Nothing he was willing to say about the relationship shed light on his mostly incomprehensible behavior. Even B, in his more reasonable moments, wondered what was so compelling about Penelope.

He didn't live with her, not at first—he had a room at a small residential hotel—but he saw her at least four times a week for the next two months. The pleasures were elusive, though he missed her the odd days they were apart. Their relationship had an indefinable quality—it was constantly improving without actually getting better. She seemed to hate it when he let it be known that he doted on her. She admired cool, so he studied numbness, aspired to some higher level of insentience. —That's so cool, was her highest praise. Her idea of him, he suspected, was miles away from the anxious person he knew himself to be.

When he found out that PT had slapped Penny around (had and had been, handiwork on display), B felt obliged to confront the younger man. Confrontation had never been easy for him—it was his emotional MO to let things slide. With all that, he had a precipitous temper, which had gotten worse with the years.

PT was deceptively mild-mannered and denied emphatically that he had ever struck Penelope. —Someone's been hitting her, B said, and all the evidence points to you.

—Violence is not in my nature, PT said, raising his arm menacingly.

After PT moved out, Penelope said she couldn't afford to keep the apartment on her own, so B offered to pay half the rent.

—I'll only accept it as a loan, she said. I don't think we know each other well enough yet to live in a small place together full time.

One day she mentioned that even though there had been nothing real between them for awhile, she kind of missed PT. It was possible, it struck B, that he had been wearing a "kick me" sign all along and he had been the only one not to notice.

B stayed away for a few days after the PT confession, as if absence were the only way to keep his tattered dignity intact. He secretly hoped that making himself scarce would raise his value on the market. His absence was also her absence. He could do without her less than she could do without him.

—Did you miss your Penny? she asked him the next time they got together. They were sitting in his parked car on a well-traveled country road.

—Penny who? he said, and that was when he found out she had no sense of humor. His remark made her cry and he loathed the oaf—himself—who had brought her pain. She refused to be comforted, pushed his hands away.

—It was a joke, he said.

—Not very funny, she told him when she could find her voice.

After they made love, she confessed that she hadn't really been hurt by his remark, knew it was a joke all the time.

—Then why the tears? he asked her.

—I wanted to get a rise out of you, she said. I wanted to see what you would do if I cried. Her revisionist confession, whether true or not, left an aftertaste of distrust.

Not all of what is known of B's liaison with Penny comes from B himself. A longtime friend, S, also a poet, though of larger reputation than B, showed up in Seattle on the last leg of a reading tour during that period (his live-in girlfriend Laura along for the whatever) and he looked up B and the two couples spent some time together.

S's initial impression of Penny was virtually the opposite of B's. He thought her passive-aggressive and subtly manipulative.

—She needs attention, was the phrase he used. Of course S tended to be ironic about even the smallest things.

When S arrived in Seattle, B was sleeping over at Penny's place virtually seven nights a week—Penny's wishes, not B's, apparently the determining factor. They had dinner together at this four star Japanese restaurant in downtown Seattle and S was in great form, his charm in fifth gear. Laura, who'd seen his act too many times before, was impatient with him, but Penny was enthralled. S's main topic of conversation was himself, but he did it in a slightly self-deprecating way, acknowledging his narcissism with some embarrassment but also going with it unashamedly, almost ingenuously because what the hell, he was who he was.

People he just met, people he hardly knew, it didn't matter their age or sex, tended to bring out the best (or worst) of his act. He tended to feel aggrieved if the least of his audience didn't love him wholeheartedly.

Anyway, after dinner they went to Penny's place for coffee and dessert. B was low-keyed through much of the evening, a witness to the events around him, content to let S have the stage. He was not jealous of S, or not so he let himself know, pleased for the most part that his friend and his inamorata were hitting it off. Of the group, only Laura seemed annoyed by S's compulsively overbearing behavior.

And then, for no apparent reason, Penny picked a fight with B in front of the others. That was later. That was during the last stages of the evening.

It was already closing in on one a.m. and Laura and S showed no signs of terminating the evening. Perhaps they were still on eastern time and thought it was already tomorrow. Perhaps they were waiting for some kind of natural closure and it may have been Penny's empathic sense of things that brought her to initiate this seemingly gratuitous fight with B. —Would you like some more brandy? B asked Laura, who had just drained her glass. —There isn't any more, Penny said and Laura said that was okay, she really didn't need anymore, and then B took his own glass, which was about half full and poured the contents into Laura's glass.

—What are you doing? Penny said in an unnaturally harsh voice. Laura doesn't want brandy from your glass, which has all these finger smudges on it. Why are you being so stupid? She smiled kittenishly at the others.

B, challenged by Penny's vehemence, withheld the urge to strike back. —Chill, he said, which was her word, giving it back to her in an ironic context like the mock return of an unwanted gift.

—I'm so sorry this happened, she said to Laura

—That's all right, Laura said, averting her eyes.

—What you did, Penny said, throwing him a sly censorious glance, was distasteful to Laura and embarrassing to me. Okay?

—Please, Laura said, leave me out of this.

B tended to be turned on by Penny's officiousness, and waited in a state of barely controlled horniness for S and Laura to go back to their hotel. The moment he got them out the door, Penny broke into tears, throwing herself face down on the bed. B sat down on the side of the bed and stroked her hair, his swollen horn pointing toward the wall, a divining rod on a false errand. When Penny was able to speak again—her grief seemed temporarily bottomless—she thanked B for his ministrations, said she didn't know what she'd do without him.

Forgiven (he assumed), he turned to embrace her. Then she said she really needed to be alone, would he mind going to his own place for what remained of the night. Of course he minded (why wouldn't he?) though he accepted his banishment with tight-lipped good grace. He didn't whine or plead, though was sorely tempted.

It was S who told B about what happened after B left, about his assignation with Penny, the whole shameful story. This was several months down the road. After S's confession, B was unforgiving, would have nothing to do with his celebrated friend for the longest time.

Penny's version of the story was different from S's. S had called, she said, about six in the morning, moments after she had at long last fallen asleep. He was complimentary, said she had the most beautiful eyes he had ever seen up close, and invited her to have breakfast with him at the Sinclair Hotel. She refused initially, but he cajoled her into coming along. B acknowledged that S could be extremely persuasive.

They had breakfast together, then he invited her to see his room, which he said was very unusual. The room was like most hotel rooms, but of course his saying the room was unusual was just an excuse to get her there. Anyway, all they did in the room was talk. He was extremely gentlemanly. Not only did they not go to bed (in her version of what happened), the question never came up.

—Had he asked, B asked her, what would you have said?

She worried the question in her ingenuous way. —I don't know, she said, taking his hand. I don't want to lie to you.

—You don't know?

—Gee, I hope I would have said no.

He believed her, he wanted to believe her, he could do nothing else but believe her. As a reward for his credulousness, she seduced him or more exactly let him seduce her. Although she had tired of him, she was unable to let him go.

Some months had passed and B was back in New York, was at the Guggenheim Museum to see the Lichtenstein show. On the fifth level, looking down at the panorama of surfaces, he noticed S a level and a half below. He thought a meeting might be awkward so he dawdled, pored over each image, deconstructed each painting with time-consuming concentration. Such attention inevitably has its own unexpected rewards, secrets offering themselves like dreams. B was zoning out on an aspect of a woman's face when he felt a large hand claim his arm.

—How are you doing, buddy? S said warmly as if there hadn't been bad blood between them, no unreconciled rift. It was as if the painting B had been staring at had yielded S from behind its blandly mysterious surface.

The men had lunch together in the Museum cafeteria. S talked of a movie he had been commissioned to write, a children's book he agreed to do in collaboration with a famous illustrator, shared news of mutual friends. After a second glass of wine, he mentioned that he and Laura had split-up which was a sad business particularly to him. B, who was in the midst of a dry period, confided little, asked questions which S tended to ignore.

—Whatever happened to that little vixen in Seattle? S asked at some point in one of his ironic modes.

It was B's turn to be evasive. —We're still in touch, he said.

—What do you mean in touch? he asked. Correspondence? Phone calls? Red-eye flights?

—Whatever, B said. What's Laura doing?

—We're not in touch, S said, except sometimes. He smiled to acknowledge the good nature behind his parody of B's evasiveness. Then he said—it was superbly timed—that he had seen B's latest novel and thought it...a brave and daring piece of work. Just before they separated, S gave B Laura's number and suggested he give her a call. —She's always liked you, he said.

—She'll be much better for you than that nut case in Seattle.

Penny had been cool to him on the phone and B felt some kind of reassuring gesture needed to be made. Two hours after he completed his poetry workshop at Columbia, he flew to Seattle, calling Penny from Kennedy and leaving a message which included estimated time of arrival on her machine minutes before boarding.

She wasn't there to meet his flight, as he had hoped, and he sat around the airport for a few hours, unable to make a decision as to what to do next. Depression sat on his chest, took the starch out of his legs. He sat in the waiting room, reading a magazine, as if waiting to meet himself.

B

After a while, he roused himself from his torpor and found a phone. His last best hope was that she wasn't there. The line was busy. So she wasn't in transit, caught in traffic, obstructed in some unavoidable way from reaching him; she was on the phone chatting with someone, some other guy most likely. She had no women friends.

Another airline had a flight from Seattle to New York that was already boarding and B, with new found urgency, decided to exchange his ticket for the more immediate return, the transaction taking its time, requiring additional funds, the confirmation of a reluctant supervisor. Nevertheless, he got to the gate in time, sweating for his efforts, and returned home 14 hours and change after his departure.

There was a message from Penny waiting for him on his answering machine. –I do want to see you, it said, but this is not the greatest time for me. Could you make it next week instead. I hope this reaches you in time. Instead of erasing the message, which was his first impulse, he tore the machine from its moorings and threw it against the wall. When in cooler heat he managed to reattach the machine, Penny's unwanted message repeated itself.

His motor still running, too exhausted to sleep, he called Laura at the number S had given him and asked her if she'd like to meet for a drink. –That would be nice, she said. Why don't you call me early next week and we'll set something up.

–I was thinking of tonight, B said. Is that not possible?

Laura laughed. –You don't waste any time, do you? Why don't you just come here? I have some interesting leftovers in the fridge. Does the idea of leftovers make you crazy?

–I often feel like a leftover myself, B said.

He arranged to see her at ten which was an hour and twenty minutes down the road, but when the time came to leave he was asleep on the couch in front of a made for TV movie about a kidnapped child. He dreamed of looking for a cab to get to Laura's and being unable to find one that was either unoccupied or disposed to stop for him.

Fortunately, the ringing of the phone woke him from his evil dream, the third or fourth ring, the machine—his voice on the machine—announcing his remote presence. The next voice was

Penny's. —Where are you, baby? it crooned. I miss you terribly, I do, believe it. I surely do. I miss you so much. I want you to consider....The time limit on the answering machine cut her off.

I won't be jerked around, B said to himself, though he called Penny back, and got—would you believe it?—a busy signal on the other end. So instead of flying back to Seattle, which he had been prepared to do, he took a cab to Laura's Chelsea area apartment.

Though Laura looked like a model (and indeed had even been briefly a model) and was smart and gifted, B had no romantic interest in her, which was odd, which was in opposition to his history. Anyway, all Laura seemed to want to talk about was S. In the course of things, B got another perspective on the events surrounding S's assignation with Penny. Returning to their hotel in a cab, Laura and S had a mild argument about S's showing off and dominating the conversation during their visit. She made what seemed to her the gentlest of complaints—it was not as if they hadn't had this conversation before. S took exaggerated exception to her remarks, responded with inappropriate vehemence. —If you think I'm so awful, S said, you could always stay at your sister's. Laura's sister lived in Bellevue, which was a nearby suburb, and Laura took the bait, found that she was angrier at S than she had original suspected.

As soon as she got to her sister's place, it struck her that S had gotten her out of the way so that he could spend the night with "Thing," which was her name for anyone whose name it pleased her not to remember. How did she know that S was with the girl? She just knew—it was S's history to do stuff like that. Anyway, when she returned the next morning to their hotel to get her clothes, S was gone. There was the name of another hotel written on a pad next to the phone. In the course of her researches—she wanted to know exactly what she was dealing with—she discovered that it was "Thing" not S who had taken a room at this other hotel. That didn't exonerate S in her view. It only meant that what had gone on was somewhat more complicated than she initially thought.

—So we're both victims, Laura said.

—And we're both also to blame for what happened, B said. B didn't like to think of himself as a victim.

—Do you really think that? Laura asked. Or are you just saying that to be clever?

—All I meant is, you want to live your life as if you're responsible for what happens to you. It sounded too pat, as he said it, and he found himself skeptical of his own wisdom.

—Even if you're really not, she said, smiling. No, I know what you mean. It was our choice, sort of, to be with untrustworthy people, wasn't it?

—Perhaps, we had no choice, he said, in the way, say, an addict has no choice.

—Speak for yourself, buddy, she said. We had a choice—at least I did....You don't really think you're addicted to Ms. Thing, do you?

—In a way, B said.

Laura came over to where he was sitting and rested her forehead against his. —No you don't, she said.

B ended up spending the night at Laura's, though neither would say what actually happened between them. Whatever, it was not a relationship that had legs, as they say.

In any event, two days later B got a cryptic phone call from S. —You're the last one I expected to pull a stunt like that, he said in an uninflected voice. Is that your idea of friendship?

B would have said, —What? which would not have raised the level of discourse if S hadn't hung up the phone on his protracted momentary silence.

After that, B stopped answering his phone. His answering machine spoke on repeated occasions to Penny, her messages becoming increasingly passionate. —Don't you know I love you? she whispered on the most recent one. He felt like a reformed alcoholic in the early stages of withdrawal or like Ulysses resisting the sirens. At some point, he not only didn't answer his phone but erased his messages without listening to them. That regimen lasted two days.

It was not so much that he forgot about her as that whenever she came to mind, and he felt the aching pull of her absence, he thought of her betrayal of him with S which short circuited his longing. He had a number of self-preserving tricks.

He threw her letters away—there were three in six months—

without opening them. He was being cowardly, he told himself, but hey, so what. Days later, in fits of courage, he would scour the garbage in the vain hope of recovering one of the banished letters.

Matters of the heart, no one had to tell B, were never clear cut. But one morning he woke up with the almost certain assurance that his fever for Penelope had all but gone. It was also that day, early in the afternoon, that B received a phone call from a familiar almost forgotten presence.

—I'm in New York, she said in her small singsong voice, dispensing with the preliminary chat, and I'd like to see you if it's possible.

It was odd how these things work. He was surely over her, but the sound of her voice sent a chill between his legs, his penis rising to salute the exorcised past. Her call, the terrifying surprise of it, caught him with his guard down. Free of her thrall or not, what harm could come of a brief meeting at a public place. The public place they agreed to meet was the Cosmos, a ratty diner across the street from the marginal low-rent hotel she had taken for the night.

She was there waiting for him in a booth in the back, dressed all in black, her complexion mottled, her long hair compacted in an oddly shaped bun, her face even gaunter than he remembered it. He could barely sense her perfume over the burnt smell of the coffee.

Penny held out her hand with awkward almost mocking formality and they shook hands. As soon as B, his hand his own again, seated himself across from her, she took his measure with a glance, nodding her head in private corroboration.

—How have you been? he asked, striking a casual tone

—How have I been? she asked herself. I've been excellent.

—Me too, he said. Excellence was having its day.

She looked like hell and was more beautiful than ever. It was a compelling combination. —What are you doing in New York? he wanted to know, wanting her to acknowledge that she couldn't keep away.

She pointed to an envelope on the table, which was the first he noticed it. —I've written a novel, she said, blushing or so it seemed (perhaps it was the light) at the admission.

His only reaction to the news was that he regretted his excessive encouragement. The two stories she had showed him in Seattle were undistinguished examples of middle of the pack undergraduate creative writing class product.

—And you've found an agent, right?, who thinks she can find a publisher for it.

—Yes. I'm kind of pleased with it, though I'd like a less self-interested opinion. She giggled.

He agreed to read the novel and give her an honest assessment of it. She thanked him for his generosity. No avowals of love were made, no offers of wild abandoned sex. There had been no need on his part for self-protective gambits. The force field of irony he kept between them had caused him to miss what was going on. He had hardly allowed himself a real look at her. On parting, she gave him a kiss on the cheek.

2.

The novel, which is called *Regrets Only*, is written in the form of a long letter from a young woman to an older man. Spare me, he thought, after he read the first two sentences. But it was reasonably compelling and after moving distractedly through the first 30 pages, he began to get caught up in the story.

The man the heroine ostensibly writes the novel to is her mother's second husband, a man she lives under the same roof with from the age of 12 to three days before her sixteenth birthday. It is difficult to tell at the outset whether her passionate letter is meant to be accusatory—a kind of this is how you ruined my life letter—or as it increasingly seems a bizarre confession of displaced love.

She starts out by apologizing (ironically?) to him for making his life "a living hell" during the time he was married to her mother. When her mother brought him to the house for the first time and introduced them his presence made such a powerful impression on her, she realized she had to keep him at a distance or she was lost. She then recounts a series of mostly petty nastinesses she pulled at his expense, and how his gentle treatment of her awfulness provoked her to raise the stakes. He never reports her to her mother, which forges a kind of bond between them. It's the bond she feels that makes her crazy, that compels her to want to destroy him. She tends to see him (his name we learn is Max) in terms of polarities. Max is either super kind or super coldhearted. One or the other. They seem almost never to talk directly to one another. It's as if he understands what it is that drives her to mistreat him. She then decides that either he is super cool or he is as infatuated with her as she is with him. If the second alternative is the true assumption, it changes everything. She begins to take notes on him in her diary as a way of figuring him out.

Max, we learn, is an actor, not always employed, who goes out auditioning for parts during the day while waiting tables several nights at week. One day the girl—she's 13 now—comes home from school and hears Max rehearsing a part (or talking to himself) in the living room, the door conspicuously ajar.

She can tell it's some kind of love scene from the few words she picks up so she stomps in as if looking for something and asks him if he'd like her to read the other part. He seems amused at her offer and no wonder, but then he says, why not, and gives her a set of cues he's typed out on two sheets of paper. It's not as much fun as reading a whole part, but she likes it well enough to continue doing it for a few more days. She's waiting for something to happen, but it doesn't look like it's going to unless she does something to make it happen. It takes awhile (the unencouraged narrator doing whatever she can to provoke), but finally she gets Max to take her in his arms (to make the scene more realistic to him) and after that the fireworks begin.

For more than two years, the narrator and her stepfather have a stormy clandestine affair, which is presented with explicit sexual detail and covers slightly more than half the length of the novel. The narrator seems less compelled by the sex (for Max the sex seems primary) than by the wary passionate obsession between them. The girl continues to be surly to Max in public, particularly in front of her mother, as a way of keeping up appearances.

Finally, during a religious crisis, Max breaks the affair off, offering, as he puts it, "a different kind of love." The narrator, furious at being discarded, fuels herself with fantasies of vengeance, including killing Max and then herself. Weeks pass and she sulks about the house, looking for a way to make Max sorry. At some point, the decision makes itself. Her mother confronts her one night when they are alone and asks her to explain her unhappiness.

—It's nothing, the girl whines. Just a phase.

—Does it have something to do with Max? the mother asks. And then prodded by her mother, she makes a seemingly reluctant accusation. Max has forced her into having sex with him. Her reluctance to inform seems to give her story, which she embellishes with each retelling, added weight. The dye is cast. Her mother seems more than willing to take her word, which is in itself gratifying. She had always felt that Max took priority over her in her mother's life. The next thing she knows Max has moved out without even saying goodbye to her. One day she asks her mother what Max has said in his defense and the mother, who seems traumatized by Max's defection, acknowledges bitterly that he made no defense.

The girl cuts her classes and begins drinking on the sly, symptoms of the larger problem. At the same time, she feels impervious to pain, secretly triumphant and powerful. At the advice of the school guidance counselor, her mother puts her into therapy. The hope is that she will work through her problems by getting in touch with her real feelings. Instead, she retells her calculated lies to the therapist, embellishing at every turn, until she begins to take at face value her own invented story. Also, by reciting the story of her abuse by an older man, she enlists sympathy from her listener, invites needed attention. There is pained tenderness in the eyes of her therapist when she recounts the abuse she suffered at her stepfather's hands.

And then, in an understated scene, she seduces her therapist. The remainder of the novel deals with a succession of affairs she has with much older men, the bouts of drinking, the overwhelming sense of undefined loss, the abortive suicide attempt. When she sees Max in a television commercial—this during a stay at substance abuse hospital—she breaks down and cries, the first tears she has shed in years. She recognizes that she has never stopped loving Max. Out of this realization, she writes the letter that comprises the novel.

The novel altered to a great extent B's sense of Penny, as in that instant when a processed photo negative suddenly presents itself with undeniable clarity. He called her almost immediately—he had read the entire manuscript in two extended readings—just moments after he scribbled the last of his notes to himself concerning it. –I've read your book, he said.

–Well, she said, did you just love it? Should I burn it and throw myself on the fire?

–It knocked me off my pins, he said.

–Whatever that means, she said. Do you want to talk to me about it? I can come by later tonight if that's all right.

By this time—the book had moved him to another place in regard to her—B had forgotten his vows to keep his distance. He suggested, his manner teacherly, she come by (it was now 8:25) around eleven.

Penny arrived in her black outfit at two minutes before midnight and B, who had been dozing, arose from the grave of his dream to unlatch the door. After she refused his ritual offer of a glass of wine, he took out his notes and read them to her, elaborating as necessary. Penny listened distractedly, changing her seat from time to time, sucking on a finger.

–You're so sexy when you're being smart, she said.

3.

She stayed the night in his bed, coiled around him like a snake. He lived in her cunt as if it were the Garden of Eden, memorizing it so he would never forget the smell or the magic of the terrain.

In the morning over breakfast, he asked her if she wanted to hear any more about her book.

–It doesn't matter, she said. Hell, I'm not going to publish it. I wrote it for you. It's the story of my tacky life.

B nodded, speechless. Hadn't he understood that that was the case all along? –It's a terrific book, he said. In the evening, he took her in a cab to the airport and waited with her for her plane to arrive. She gave him a chaste peck on the cheek before she slithered through the metal detector. After that, he took an escalator up to the observatory and watched her plane ascend. Her smell hung about him like an invisible embrace. As he left the airport and took a cab home, her musky aura rehearsed itself in memory, echoed its pleasure. As he rode in unyielding traffic through the Midtown Tunnel, horns blaring in discordant chorus, he had a sense of extraordinary well being. He was, for a rare moment, poet-in-residence in his own skin. It wouldn't matter to B now, not a lot, not everything, if he never saw or spoke to Penny again. Which meant they could remain friends or whatever it was they were. The feverish component of the relationship, the unappeasable sexual heat, had passed. It was that, the near unbearable joy of their night together in his New York bed, that brought a satisfying closure to the story. He could write about it now, and would, he could take it or leave it. Closure released one from debilitating obsession. Anyway, that was the myth B brought home with him to his lonely apartment.

VII. HEARTBREAK ANONYMOUS

1.
B was in the throes of mourning or something worse, some incalculable sorrow, some persistently free-floating grief. He managed no more than three hours of sleep a night, woke in the dark with this ache of loss like a computer virus scrawling its indecipherable demons across the page of his soul. B went to bed when exhaustion wore through his resistance to sleep with the same unabated grief hanging out within. It had no source or at least none he could identify and say this person, this woman, this lost love, is the cause of my pain.

It was seven years now since I had separated from Genevieve with whom I had lived (while sometime married) for 18 years. It seemed like longer than that, it seemed like the illusion of forever. There had been a few women in my life, a handful or so, since the breakup of my marriage, and though I had been in love with some of them, none had lasted long enough to leave behind this weight of loss in her wake. Perhaps it was all of them together I grieved for or perhaps it was Rebecca, the last in line, the one who reminded me most of Genevieve.

If Rebecca's absence from my life was the cause of my

suffering, there was remedy at hand. I could just call her up and arrange to see her, which I thought of doing only long enough to conjure the last maddening days of our relationship. The more I obsessed about my situation, the less susceptible it was to being understood. When these feelings of loss persisted like one of those perpetual nagging colds New Yorkers seem to get, I had a medical examination (which revealed only that my resistance was down) and visited a succession of user-recommended shrinks. My medical doctor advised an exercise regimen, running or swimming or cycling, and gave me a prescription for an antidepressant. In the spirit of trying anything, I took the drug for a few weeks, and felt somewhat better, the ache still there but velvety and distant.

The shrinks—there was really only one—made a point of not offering advice, wanted me to work through whatever it was, which meant telling her about my relationship to my mother—my non-relationship—that can of worms.

I got on fine with my mother, I said. It was what I always said about her. She was a bit remote, though unrelentingly supportive. No telling details offered themselves. As a last resort, though otherwise unclubbable, I attended meetings of a group called Heartbreak Anonymous, which I had seen advertised in the Personals section of *The Village Voice*. Meetings were held Wednesday nights at a downtown church immediately after the Alanon session was concluded. I sensed an obvious difference between my situation and that of most of my fellow heartbreak sufferers. Everyone at the meeting seemed to know exactly who the heartbreaker was that had reduced them to their present tormented state. The purpose of the group was to help the heartbroken root out obsession with the lost beloved. Members chalked up the days in which they didn't obsess about winning back the one for whom they grieved. On this score, I was out of the loop. My treacherous ghost, whoever, had neither name nor face.

H.A. (the insiders name for it) did not fail B altogether. At the end of the third meeting, he struck up a conversation with a lively faded beauty with the face of a Fra Angelico Madonna and offered

B

her a ride home in his car. The woman, H, invited him in for a drink or whatever and they ended up doing the whatever, behavior directly contrary to strictures for H.A. members of less than 60 days standing.

—This has been so good for me, she said just after the minor aria of her orgasm had had its moment on stage. You'll notice, I didn't once mention Phillip's name.

—You didn't, he acknowledged, until now.

—Usually when I'm with a guy, I end up talking about Phillip, which gets a lot of guys pissed at me. It's different with you. You don't even remind me of Phillip except in the eyes. Phillip's eyes are the same shade of blue.

When B was ready to leave, retiring the half-finished cup of coffee she had insisted on making for him, she lowered her eyes shyly and asked if they would ever see each other again.

The question flustered him. —I'll call you, he heard himself saying as if the answer had been waiting on his tongue almost forever.

H smiled sadly, gave him a skeptical look. He assured her again that he would be in touch. Wary of commitment, he was glad to get away.

For all that, he felt almost okay (despite the ticket on his windshield) after he retrieved his car and made the long drive home. The grief in residence, that persistent uninvited guest, seemed to have gone off on an unannounced trip.

The liaison with H had done B some good and he wanted to call her the next day to tell her so, but he couldn't find her number anywhere. He could barely remember her giving it to him, though it was possible he had forgotten to take the piece of note paper she had written it on.

I went to the next H.A. meeting at the All Soul's Church, expecting (though not quite hoping) to run into Helena. Her absence from the meeting disappointed me more than I imagined possible. My inquiries produced raised eyebrows. No one seemed to know anything about her. Helena's last meeting, for all anyone knew, might have been her first.

I continued to feel improved, found myself whistling in the shower one morning, felt almost functional. Two weeks of H.A. meetings passed without Helena in attendance and it bothered me that she would think I had reneged on my promise to call.

So, one Saturday afternoon, stuck on the story I had been fiddling with for six months and was about ready to discard, I drove to Helena's place on Amsterdam Avenue to let her know why she hadn't heard from me. I missed her, I told myself, though of course I barely knew who she was.

No one seemed to be home and I made several tries, hanging around the neighborhood for over an hour, then going to a local movie before trying again to no avail. It wasn't so much that I was desperate to see her—it was and it wasn't—as that I wanted to do the right thing.

I worried that something had happened to Helena, that she had gotten sick or done herself some harm.

Still, busyness, the usual distractions (plus a new one, a new woman in my life), kept me from her door for another two weeks. This time I was in luck: I caught her leaving the building just as I was pulling up in my car. She looked even sadder than the saintly image of her that flickered from time to time in my untrustworthy memory. Helena positively glowed with grief.

When I called to her from the car, she ignored me and continued walking at an increased pace. I would have cruised alongside her, but there was a stopped cab just in front of me trapping me in place.

Not wanting to risk losing her again, I abandoned the car in the middle of the street and jogged after her, catching up as she was about to descend the subway steps.

—I was calling you, I said. Didn't you hear me?

—Please go away, she said. You're making a scene.

—I need to talk to you, I said. Will you come back to the car with me? I couldn't find your number and I didn't know how to get in touch.

—I'm no longer available to you, she said, her hand over her heart, a touch of melodrama in her voice. You've had your chance and you've thrown it away.

I stared after her as she hurried down the steps, her heels clicking like castanets, then I fled back to my car. A policeman was waiting for me with one of the aggrieved drivers trapped behind me. The cop had already started writing the ticket so there was nothing I could say to influence him.

I pleaded the vagaries of love. The snitch, who had called the cop, smirked with satisfaction as the cop, all business, handed me my ticket.

That evening, out for dinner with V, the new woman in his life, B told the story of the officious citizen who had turned him into the police because he had left his car for a moment when it had been stuck behind a cab. V said that anyone who called the police on someone because of a moment's inconvenience was beneath contempt. B thought so too, though he suspected her sympathy was worked-up.

He didn't mention H and invented another reason for having left his car.

The next morning when the ache of loss returned from wherever it had strayed, its intensity undiminished, B knew that it was H's absence he suffered and H's absence alone. His free-floating grief had found its object.

—You seem inconsolable, sweetheart, Vivian said to me over dinner, to which I nodded in acknowledgment. I had done everything in my power to avoid obsessing about Helena and had failed miserably.

—I'm fine, I said irritably.

—I've seen you better, she said.

A minor disagreement emerged which had the earmarks of a fight. If it was what it seemed, it was our first, a landmark perhaps or the beginning of the end. I was in one of those curmudgeonly moods that seeks out trouble. In thrall to my discontent, I went home at midnight, though it was my custom (of two weeks) to spend Saturday nights at Vivian's place. The inconsolable, it was mutually agreed, were best left to sulk in their own tents of residence unattended.

I found two messages waiting for me at home on my answering machine. One from Vivian regretting our fight and one from Helena pleading for forgiveness for her "unforgivable behavior." Helena left her number for my reply, the number coming through in garbled form and I had to play the message back several times to make almost sure I had it right. It was close to one a.m. and I fretted about whether it was acceptable to call so late.

By this point, I kind of believed we were fated not to connect—that I had the number wrong or she would be out—so that when she answered on the first ring I was at a loss for something to say. —I just got home, I said, and found your message waiting for me.

—Where were you? she said, a subtext of disappointment in the question.

—I was visiting a friend, I said. Look, I've done nothing but think about you since that night we met.

—What were you doing with this friend? she asked. I ignored the question which I thought unworthy of her, reiterated my desire to see her again as soon as possible.

—If you wanted so much to see me, why were you out with this friend? she asked.

It was like a bad dream in which the other person was speaking a seemingly familiar language that made little or no sense. Perhaps she was being slyly amusing and I had failed to pick up on the joke.

—When my first choice isn't available, I said, I sometimes take the next best offer.

—I suppose you think I'm out of line asking but I have a history of getting involved with men who are already taken. Are you already taken?

I was in one of those double-bind situations where I wanted to tell the truth, but at the same time didn't want to discourage.

—I'm not taken, I said, italicizing the taken in my mind,

though I have been dating someone. I was aware of feeling in danger as I waited for her delayed response.

—Well, she said, if you come over now, I'm going to expect you to stay the night. I want to get that out so there's no misunderstanding later.

—Why don't we do this tomorrow night, I said. I'll take you to dinner and we'll see how things go.

—You don't want to see me tonight? she asked.

—It's kind of late, isn't it? I'd like to see you tonight, but we both need to get some sleep, don't you think?

—I don't sleep much, she said. Anyway I'm busy tomorrow night.

She was also—I pursued alternatives—busy the next night and the night after that. —Are you saying, I asked, that if I don't come over tonight, you don't want to see me at all?

—Look, do you want to come over or don't you? I had the impression from the way you ran after me yesterday that you were dying to see me. If I've misinterpreted, we can just say good-bye and avoid getting into something we'll both eventually regret.

Alarms went off in my head, which I did my unsuccessful best to ignore. —Look, I'll call you tomorrow, I said.

—That's if you don't lose my number first, she said in a low, pained voice, and that was it.

She called back in the morning to apologize for her edginess. She talked about having been hurt in a long-term relationship and how long, as someone like me had to know, such hurts took to heal. I commiserated, forgave her, dredged up my own apology.

B spent the next few months seeing H at least once a week, sleeping over on Friday nights—the sex sometimes spectacular—comforting her when a sudden recollection of Phillip's defection would throw her into paroxysms of grief. Her presence, her operatic affection, were his comfort. They attended H.A. meetings together on Wednesday evenings, sometimes holding hands out of sight of the others.

B continued to see V on occasion, keeping her a secret from H, who was intensely jealous. When B found a free moment to think about it, it troubled him that his life had become so busy and complicated, so fraught with potential dangers, he had virtually no time to sit in front of the computer and imagine language on a blank screen. H was becoming increasingly demanding. The more time B spent with her, the more jealous she became of the life he lived outside her company.

So B had to know he was asking for trouble when he told her that as much as he appreciated her company he needed more time to himself. At first H accepted the news well, said that she could understand as a writer he needed extended periods of time to collect his thoughts.

B said he was grateful for the generosity of her response and warming toward her, he remembered the terrible ache of loss he once felt at her absence. Love revisited and he put his arms around H, holding her against him, lifting her into the air. After they kissed (H had this way of bruising her lips against his) he carried her into the bedroom like a bride. H was a clothes designer and the bookcase headboard of her custom-made platform bed was filled with copies of *Vogue, Elle, Mirabella* and *Vanity Fair*. Perfume seemed to emanate from the magazines.

After they made love, H confided that it bothered her just a little that his writing was more important to him than she was. He had no choice but to write, he told her. Not writing for him was not being alive.

—You poor man, she said, kissing his face. All her gestures tended to excess.

At two in the morning she woke him to say that she felt unbearably unhappy and that he was the cause.

—What did I do wrong? he asked, still half asleep, trying to remember details from the dream that was slipping away.

—If you have to ask that question, she said, I think I'd like you to get your things together and leave.

—I'm sorry I made you unhappy, he said, turning on his side away from her. Can we discuss this in the morning?

—If that's what you want, she said, but before he could reclaim his dream, the light was on and she was shaking him.

—In my space, I'm the one who makes the decisions, she said.

To argue with her as he knew from two previous occasions was to make her even more adamant so he got out of bed and began to get dressed in a desultory way.

As B was letting himself out she said, —If you had any character, you wouldn't let a woman bully you this way. Phillip would have smacked me one if I dared to mouth off to him.

—Phillip's footprints are too large for me to fill, B said, pleased with the remark only until its cheapshotness registered in private echo.

First B couldn't remember where he parked his car and when he found it on Riverside Drive the radiator grill was gone, had apparently been blown loose by the heavy winds. He wandered up and down the block looking for the errant part, persecuted by the cold, cursing the fates. It was like a piece of him had blown off into the abyss.

When I got home, there was a message from Helena waiting for me on the answering machine.

—I never want to see you again, it said. Who the fuck do you think you are?

The ringing of the phone woke me some hours later, the room filled with light, and I staggered from bed to answer. I was in one of my curmudgeonly moods.

The voice at my ear pleaded for forgiveness.

—I wish it were in me, I said, still angry at my banishment. I'll call you when I'm ready.

—You will never forgive me, she said with a certitude I found hard to dispute.

2.

B wasn't sure whether the indefinable sorrow that had been haunting him had gone away or that it had become so familiar he had grown to accept it as a natural condition. Or perhaps his bruised feelings had produced a protective covering. Whatever, the pain he had once thought irremediable seemed barely a glimmer of its former self. It was as though he had dreamed of loss and woke to find he had everything he could possibly want.

B had become less quixotic in his passions. He no longer fell in and out of love precipitously, but chose his companions in a clear-eyed and sensible way. An unfamiliar calm had come over him. His worries seemed unimportant, his chronic discontents a parody that at long last began to entertain, his former loneliness an aspect of the unremembered past. Whereas his emotional life had been a muddle from the outset, he made useful distinctions now between sexual need and emotional entanglement. Both in this age of disease carried their own unacceptable baggage. All of his past loves, it struck him, had been prohibitively difficult puzzles he had predictably failed to solve.

B had entered a period of post-storm calm. He had a brief obsessive affair with a 20-year-old he had met in Seattle on a reading tour.

In his present becalmed state, he could barely imagine what had attracted him to H in the first place or to R for that matter or to G, for whose loss he had grieved for what seemed like years. Of the three, only H remained a continuing (though remote) presence in his life. They no longer dated—the night she threw him out of her apartment had brought an end to that phase of their relationship—but they bantered on the phone from time to time and occasionally got together for lunch. The calls generally came from H and it struck him that if she stopped calling, their friendship, if that's what it was, would come to an irrevocable end.

Months had passed since our last conversation and I began to concern myself in some distant way about Helena, worrying that she had lost her job or gotten sick or gone back to the Midwest. I remembered that during our last conversation she had mentioned going for a checkup to a doctor she had never been to before. She had been anxious about it, had been dwelling on certain real or imaginary symptoms. And then I had this disturbing dream in which Helena called to tell me she was dying of a rare, recently discovered, sexually transmitted disease.

I called the next day and a recording reported that her number was no longer in service. My follow-up call produced predictably the same result. We had no friends in common and I let myself believe there was no way of finding out where she might have gone. And even if there was a way, what possible good would it do me to know. Instead of thinking about Helena, I focused on feeling nothing, nurtured the frail sense of well being that lately sustained me.

A few weeks after the dream, impelled by an unfocused urgency, I drove to her building and rang the superintendent's buzzer. A frightened painfully thin Chinese woman appeared at the door.

–My husband out, she said, eyeing me suspiciously.

–Do you know what happened to the woman in 3B? I asked.

–My husband back in one hour, she said, holding up two fingers to signify. You come back.

Though I could see the super's wife was uncomfortable with strangers, I resisted dismissal. –The woman in 3B, I asked, did she leave a forwarding address? The super's wife, who seemed careworn and tired, stared blankly at me.

–Husband back in one hour, she said.

I spoke slowly, rephrasing my question, emphasizing each word.

A small light went on in her tired eyes. –You want to see apartment? she asked and the next thing I knew I was following the woman up the stairs. A child of three or four tagged along behind us.

After she had ushered me into the apartment, the woman picked up the child and stood waiting like a sentry by the opened door. I checked out each of the four rooms that comprised Helena's former flat, performing the role assigned me as prospective renter. The place had been cleaned and cleaned out, though a few odds and ends of furniture remained, including the newish platform bed we had slept in together the six or seven times I had spent the night.

Suddenly weary, I plopped myself down on the bed—it was the only place in the bedroom to sit. Though it was an okay apartment, and showed well even without Helena's few well chosen things, I recognized that there was something sad about its emptiness, a sadness I could not or would not feel. I lay back on the bed with my hands pillowed behind my head and closed my eyes. Dozing was not part of my agenda. I meant only to collect myself before leaving to go home.

My mind was abuzz, my senses heightened. I was aware of a slight medicinal smell in the room, bare traces of illness. That's when I thought of renting the flat and keeping it for Helena in case someday she wanted to return from wherever she had gone, though I couldn't really afford to keep two apartments. Nevertheless I held on to the sentimental idea, played with it in my imagination as if I were a character in a made-up story. Then I found myself thinking of a time I had visited my mother in the hospital and she had not recognized me, had not the faintest idea who I was. Even after I introduced myself and she smiled warmly at me, I could tell she remained skeptical about my credentials and had drawn on resources of graciousness to get through a potentially embarrassing situation. She pretended to know me and I went along with the pretense because it seemed the only acceptable choice.

Then I remembered my father telling me that if I had been more attentive to my mother, she never would have lost her memory. Then I remembered looking at Genevieve's diary, which seemed to have been left about for my discovery. The entry that caught my eye made me regret my intrusion. –I realized this morning, it read, that I don't love B. When I look back on it now, I don't think I ever loved him.

Then I remembered my father, who had these crazy moments, informing me in a letter that he no longer thought of me as his son.

I was beyond being hurt by these memories. I took my antidepressant twice daily, after breakfast and before going to bed. Nothing touched me these days, not much, not deeply, and not, so I thought, more in despair than hope, ever again.

B

The super's wife came into H's bedroom and said something to B in Chinese, something harsh apparently, her eyes angry, perhaps worried. He figured she was asking him to leave, which he had every intention of doing, but for some reason he didn't move, was not quite ready to make the effort. That wasn't it exactly. His spirit had already taken the necessary steps, had risen from the bed, had thanked the woman for showing him the apartment, had returned to his car, which had a popped lock on the driver's side and an open space where the tape deck had been, had started up the car and driven through the usual relentless traffic to his parking garage, had walked the two plus blocks to his co-op apartment (his home, his safe place), opening both locks and closing them again from the inside, making himself a Scotch and water, putting a Kronus Quartet CD on the player, remoting on the TV without sound, lying down on the couch, calling up from the deep an opening sentence for the impending story about H he somehow needed to tell. That sentence, the first he had conjured in a long time, gave him a sense of justification, kept the demons on their best behavior.

    The super's wife sat down next to B on H's bed and patted his hand.

    —You be all light, she said.

VIII. OBLIGATIONS

An unpostmarked letter arrives for B—it has been folded over and jammed into his mail slot—which opens with the sentence, –As of this moment, you are no longer my son. The letter is unsigned but the handwriting is unmistakably that of the man who is in a position to issue such a renunciation.

What has he done now, what can he possibly have done, to provoke the old man to this extreme?

Two days before, he had taken his aged parents with a realtor friend to look at some co-ops with the idea of having them move from their four story brownstone to a place that didn't require climbing stairs. His father had seemed offended that none of the apartments he was shown was as grand as the house he was apparently being asked to give up, but he was on his best behavior with the realtor, who was an attractive young woman, and she told B afterward that his father was one of the most charming older men she'd ever met.

For his part, B said next to nothing during the tour. He knew from a lifetime of failed attempts to urge his father to anything was to invite resistance. His mother, who had lost all immediate memory, had become no more than a bystander to the decisions made concerning her. Her constant question, asked the moment she forgot she had been already answered, was –What do I do now? To which his father would answer sententiously, –Whatever it is, darling, it doesn't matter because you're already doing it.

When they were tired of walking through other people's rooms, he drove his parents home and he parted with his father, or so it seemed, on friendly terms.

Shortly after the vexing letter arrives, B phones the woman he's been seeing off and on to report his grievance in a slightly amused, studiedly casual way. She isn't home and doesn't answer at work so he goes through his address book looking for some other low-maintenance sympathetic listener.

His father's letter is like having a curse on his head and until it is removed, his only concern is easing the trauma. His day is filled with negligible incident: he takes an extended morning walk, has a pre-lunch beer, reads student work, adds a few sentences to a story he has been working on, holds unscheduled office hours at the college. Still the only thing on his mind is his father's renunciation and he rehearses the opening sentence to himself as if it weren't already etched indelibly in memory. When a colleague from the college calls on a professional matter, he finds himself telling her of his father's angry letter.

—How awful for you, she says, and then proceeds to tell him of the tyrannies of her own parents, her mother forcing her to eat for breakfast whatever she left over from dinner the night before.

—Why aren't our parents as smart as we are, he says.

His sharing of his father's letter with this stranger eases his burden only for the duration of the call. They talk of meeting some evening for dinner to continue their newfound intimacy. He promises that whatever food she leaves over will go back to the kitchen and disappear from her life forever.

B returns to a psychotherapist who had pronounced him graduated from what had been a five year analysis six months ago. The therapist, Henrietta Doan, seems disappointed by what is obviously a regression in his behavior as if her judgment in releasing him were at fault. His father, she reminds him, feels disempowered and that makes him want to strike out at those he feels are usurping his prerogatives.

B understands and yet only up to a point, comes away from his therapy unimproved. Though the sun is out, a dark cloud hangs over his head, trailing him like an aura of the defeated. He keeps the letter a secret for the most part, embarrassed by the madness of his father's gesture. Sometimes he breaks up laughing at his private melodrama. No one can possibly know how wronged I've been, he tells himself.

—I love and admire my father, B announces to his therapist, though I can't stand being around him more than forty minutes at a time. Does that make any sense?

—It sounds to me as if you hate him, she says.

He insists that she has misunderstood his remark. He searches his memory for episodes that illustrate his point, the occasions, for example, his father took him as a child on excursions to art galleries, which were one of his favorite things to do. He recalls a time they went together to a show of some prized new painter and his father made a point of explaining to B what was wrong with the work, his voice carrying, though the artist and dealer were in a huddle on the other side of the room.

—Look at this, he remembers his father declaiming as if he were lecturing to a classroom of the deaf, the man has no sense of color, the man can't draw a line.

—Dad, the mortified 11-year-old B whispered, the painter can hear you.

—Let him hear me, his father roared. Someone ought to tell him he can't paint.

That isn't the example he means to give. One anecdotal memory leads to another similar memory and B feeds on each for awhile only to distrust their unrelenting one-sidedness. Why can't he dredge up scenes of his father as the generous or affectionate person he sometimes was?

When he first started to write, his father had been encouraging, even admiring. Sometimes he let slip a negative comment after the fact of his initial praise, catching B off his guard. His father approved or mostly approved of the various women B had married. On at least two occasions, he seemed to prefer the woman B had married to B himself.

When a neighbor told the 12-year-old B that he had a walk just like his father, B had taken pleasure in the comparison. He used to baby sit for this neighbor's children and play pool on their table. The memory is strong, though he distrusts it. Now as he gets older it worries him that he is becoming the same irascible curmudgeon his father has almost always been.

In desperation B composes the following letter:

Dear Dad,

I hesitate to call you Dad since you have disclaimed me as a son, but I'm writing to you to clear up what seems a misunderstanding between us. In taking you and mom to look at co-ops, which you seemed interested in pursuing, I was not trying to push you out of your place, if that's what you think but to help you make your life more comfortable. If you don't want to move, I'm willing to let the matter drop, though you've been complaining incessantly about how difficult the stairs have been for you and mother. Perhaps you have some other imagined grievance against me and it has nothing to do with my taking you to look at apartments. I care for you and want you to be happy so I hope we can resolve this apparent crisis and return to our usual low level manageable tension. Otherwise, the hell with you.

B lets the unfinished letter sit on his desk three days before destroying it. An array of scenarios concerning his father passes through his mind unencouraged.

B

A week or so later, his father calls to ask why he hasn't heard from B.

—Come over, his father barks at him. I need to talk to you right away.

—Dad, he says, you said you didn't want to see me again.

His remark ushers in thirty seconds of dead phone time.

—When did I say that? his father asks. Who told you I said I didn't want to see you. Didn't I just this moment invite you to come over?

B sees no point in resurrecting the past particularly since his father seems to have forgotten the letter. —I'll come by tomorrow at two o'clock, he says.

—This can't wait, his father says. Son, oblige me and come over now. This concerns you. This is something that has to be discussed right away. I've been thinking about this for a long time.

—I have to be at the college in an hour, B says. It is his standard evasion these days and it evokes a heavy sigh from his father.

—I'll expect you tomorrow if it has to be tomorrow, his father says, and hangs up.

The curse on his head lifted, it is as if it has never been there or has always been there, one or the other. He feels both elated and unrelieved. B senses that the more he accedes to his father's whimsical demands, the more contempt he earns. Yet he sympathizes with the grimness of his father's situation. The old man is stuck in this huge house—he has mostly stopped painting in the last year—with nothing to do but worry about his health, which is amazingly good, and wait for his death.

B shakes off his sense of grievance and phones his father.

—Who is this? his father asks after hearing B's distinctive voice.

—Dad, B says, I can come by tomorrow between 12 and one and take you for a haircut.

—You knew I needed a haircut, his father says. That's wonderful.

—I thought it was about time, B says.

A moment of throat clearing follows. —Isn't that curious? his father says. Just last night I dreamed you called to apologize. Isn't that something? How could I have possibly known that you'd call?

—So I'll see you tomorrow, B says.

—In the dream you came over right away and didn't keep me waiting, his father says.

In his role of grudging caretaker, B drives to the Heights to visit his father, lucking into a parking spot two blocks away. As he gets out of the car, he hears his name in the air. It is the woman in his department, the one he exchanged confidences with on the phone about a week ago.

—What are you doing in my neighborhood? she asks after they have awkwardly shaken hands. She has been carrying groceries and has to shift them from her right arm to her left.

B concedes that he is visiting his parents who live a few blocks from where they stand.

—I thought your father had excommunicated you, she says. Isn't that what you told me?

B walks her to her door, which is in a mostly opposite direction from the one in which he is going, relishing the delay.

—Would you like to come in for a cup of coffee? she asks.

B glances at her—he has not really noticed her before—and registers that she is prematurely gray, is overweight, and has what might be described as a dowdy post-hippie style. She is wearing a colorful peasanty, tent-like dress that calls attention to her heaviness rather than disguises it. She has an angular, intelligent, sympathetic, not unattractive face.

—My father is expecting me, B says, which is his indirect way of accepting her invitation.

He ends up having a glass of white wine instead of coffee and the woman—Tamara—tells him an intimate story about a man she had been dating who had told her he loved her and then a week later said he thought it was best if they ended things before they went too far. She had been hurt and mystified by the man's behavior and she asks B if as a man he can explain to her what was going on from the man's point of view.

Of course B has no idea why this man he doesn't know has behaved as he had, though that doesn't stop him from marketing an opinion. –It sounds to me as if he got frightened that things were moving too quickly, he says.

–We had been dating for two years, Tamara says. That was the first time he ever told me he loved me.

He may have been seeing someone else, B thinks, and told her he loved her out of guilt and because there was no longer so much at stake. –A lot of men are afraid of intimacy, B says as if his making the comment excludes him from the universal judgment.

–He's been married before, she says, and has a 10-year-old son. He's a very loving father. I thought you might understand him because you've been through similar experiences. Have you ever broken off a relationship abruptly like that?

B had a tendency when he wanted to get out of a relationship to behave carelessly and objectionably until the woman broke it off. At that point, he usually felt mistreated and regretful and then tried to salvage matters that were beyond salvation.

–Do you know if he's seeing someone else now? B asks.

A comic strip light bulb comes on over Tamara's head.

–A few days before he ended it, he said he thought it would be a good idea if we allowed ourselves to see other people. I said I didn't know what to make of such a suggestion.

–That means he was already seeing someone else, B says, glancing surreptitiously at his watch.

–Does it? What a creep. We had always been so honest with each other, we really had. It's hard for me to accept his being so two-faced.

–Look, B says, as much as I'd rather talk to you, I'd better go and see my father. I'll stop by afterward if you want to continue this. She makes no attempt to hide her disappointment in him.

–You don't have to, she says. I'm sorry if I bored you with my problems.

–My father gets impatient, B says, which leads to rage. He may renounce me again and refuse to see me.

–I don't think so, she says. I suspect after all that waiting, he'll be extra-glad to see you. Would you like to come back?

—I'll come back, he says.

It is a promise he regrets making as soon as he is out the door.

She is right of course. His father seems more than usually pleased to see him, offers to give B the dark green cashmere jacket he is wearing that B has offhandedly admired. There is no important news his father has to impart, there never is, beyond some new ideas his father has about painting that B has heard more than once before.

His father mentions that he had picked up B's first novel and then couldn't put it down and had read more than half of it in three hours and that it was so much more "luminous" than he remembered. B knows better than to allow himself to be pleased, though some small taste of gratification filters through his guard. Then he goes upstairs with his father to his studio for a showing of new work. His father shows B some paintings he has shown B on his last visit plus some old work plus one new painting he hasn't seen.

—I can still do it, he says, can't I?

His mother who has been silent up until then laughs at his father's remark.

—Don't boast, Hudson, she whispers.

B is obligingly impressed as always, acknowledges that his 89-year-old father is as good a painter as ever, makes some willfully perceptive comments about the painting on display.

—You're my best critic, his father says. When you look at my paintings I see them anew through your eyes. His father's unrelenting compliments begin to make B tense. He is struck by the dangerous fragility of the moment and feels an urgency about getting away before his father's sweet humor disintegrates into something else.

He announces he has to be at the college to meet a class, collects his jacket, kisses his mother good-bye.

—Where are you always running off to? his father says as B approaches him. I need you around to confirm my existence. They embrace awkwardly, his father sitting in a high-back chair, B leaning over him, the muscles in his back in tortured opposition.

–I hope your children are more dutiful than mine, his father calls after B as he scoots down the stairs.

It is only after he has driven almost halfway home that B remembers his promise to Tamara to resume his visit. Since he doesn't particularly want to go back—he had no friendships with women that didn't evolve or devolve into sex—the promise hangs on him like an obligation. He notices a public phone on the next street and parks the car and walks over, thinking merely to be honest, not knowing how else to proceed.

He has to call Information to get her number but once inside the booth, her last name, which he knows perfectly well, evades memory. It is something with a G or a K, two or three syllables, a European name. There is nothing to do but go home (he has no impetus to go back) and call Tamara from there.

When he gets home there is a message on the answering machine from his father. –You forgot to take the jacket, his father says stiffly in a hoarse voice. It takes B a moment or two to figure out what jacket his father is referring to.

B is lying down, exhausted from what has been one of the most gratifying visits with his father in a long time when he remembers that he has forgotten to call Tamara Gielson. He is planning his excuses, investing them with worked-up conviction when he dozes off.

He seems to dream the call, but in the dream which is unusually lucid he gets his father on the line, having somehow dialed the wrong number.

–When are you coming over? his father asks. I have some things to tell you.

–Could you do me a favor? B asks. Could you go over to 126 Pineapple Street—he isn't even sure it is the right address—and tell this woman, Tamara, that my promise to return had completely slipped my mind?

—I need you to take me for a haircut, tomorrow, his father says. Maybe some time next week we could visit your friend together.

B entertains the idea of visiting Tamara with his father, but the timing is inappropriate. How could he wait a week to explain his failure to keep an appointment? The damage to his credibility by that time would be irrevocable. He suffers the demise of his word. The word. All words.

After he escapes his parents' house, B heads back to Tamara's garden apartment to resume his visit. It is dark out, though barely four o'clock, the streets deserted, the wind gusting, leaves float by like swarms of insects. Several minutes pass and B patiently rings the bell a second time. He looks for a card in his wallet on which to leave a note.

Finally the door opens. Tamara is wearing a dusty white terry cloth bathrobe revealing a purple slip or nightgown perhaps underneath. —You caught me napping, she says. Could you take a walk around the block and come back?

—I probably should go on home, B says. I could use a nap myself. I just wanted to let you know I hadn't forgotten my promise.

—You might as well come in and take your nap here, she says. I won't disturb you and when you wake we can continue our talk. As soon as he steps in and she closes the door behind him, she throws herself against him and they kiss open-mouthed. What's going on? He can hardly believe how excited he is by the press of her body against his, though he has not thought of her, not for a minute, not ever, in sexual terms before.

They grind and kiss and fondle one another in the living room for a few overheated minutes and then she gently pushes him away. —We don't know each other well enough for this, she says.

B feels apish hulking about in her living room with his hard-on like a teenager's advertising its intrusive presence, so he makes a nervous joke. —I thought we were getting acquainted pretty well there for awhile, he says. His arms hang awkwardly at his sides like uninvited guests.

—Do you still want to take a nap? she asks him. By this time she has created some distance between them, turning on an art deco lamp in a dark corner. I can put you up on the couch in my study.

What B wants to do is fuck—it is the only thing he has on his mind—and he struggles in vain to conceive of some other alternative. —I think I should go home now, he says.

—Oh, please! she says. Don't you think we ought to talk about what happened?

—Whatever happened, he says, working to disguise the annoyance he feels, common sense prevailed.

—You don't mean that, she says. At least say what you mean. You're angry at me for rejecting you. Admit that that's what you feel.

—Tamara, I don't know what I feel, B says. I want to go home and think about what I feel. Inertia holds him in place though he has thought about moving toward the door, which is only a few steps behind him.

—If I agreed to have sex with you, she says, then you'd stay? Is that what this is about?

This is a version of a nightmare B has had before. He watches himself studying the collection of song books in her bookcase as if some title or other might explain something. "The Dying Cowboy's Lament" holds his attention. —Stop jerking me around, he says, suddenly furious with her. I wouldn't have touched you if you hadn't come on to me first.

—I don't know where you're coming from, she says, lip quivering.

Eventually, he gets out the door, feeling twice mugged.

He promises he will call her as he makes his escape—that standard unworthy line—compounding his lies.

As he unlocks his car and eases himself into the driver's seat, he notices his father carrying a brown bag from the liquor store trudging toward him, eyes inward, lost in some private dialogue. B ducks down in his seat and waits for his father to pass, reasonably sure he has not been noticed.

Just as his father's shadow slides by, he hears his name being called, a woman's voice floating his name in the air, and B notices in his side-view mirror, Tamara coming up right behind his father, waving in B's direction as if he were a taxi she was hoping to claim. His father stops in his tracks and turns to press his face to B's window, discovering (or so B allows himself to imagine) a familiar figure hunched behind the wheel of the parked car, the ungrateful dissembler he sometimes acknowledges as his son.

B and his father walk over together to Tamara's place and B rings the bell.

—This is my father, Hudson, he says when she opens the door.

—He wants to apologize for not keeping his appointment last week, his father says. I want to tell you he does the same thing with me so you don't have to take it personally.

—It's a pleasure to meet you, Tamara.

—The pleasure's all mine, she says. I heard you were a wonderful painter, Hudson.

—Tamara, you'll have to come up to my studio one of these days and make your own judgments, his father says. I'll tell you this much, if it had been me, I would have kept my appointment to see you.

—I believe that, she says. Would you like to come in for a cup of coffee or a glass of wine?

As they talk, B feels himself growing dimmer, fading by imperceptible degrees. At some point, after his father follows Tamara into her small apartment for a glass of white wine, he disappears, sucked up into the black hole of his own space.

IX. INTIMACY

1.
The invitation came by phone on a holdover winter morning in late March and caught B musing on the opening phrase of a poem. Perhaps because the offer seemed so improbable, or perhaps merely because he was distracted, he accepted without hesitation.

The Femmes Club, an organization of previously married women, was looking for a speaker on the topic: —After Marriage, What? said his caller, a throaty-voiced woman (he assumed it was a woman though couldn't be sure), and he had been brought to the Club's attention (he couldn't imagine from what source) as a controversial authority on the subject.

–I'm flattered that you thought of me, B said, his response on automatic pilot.

–Well, to be honest, said his caller, you were not our first choice, but when our first choice became unavailable you were the unanimous selection to replace her. And now that I hear your voice I think we've got our hands on absolutely the right person.

–I'm curious to know where you got my name, he said, wondering if a new career as occasional speaker might be opening up to him.

–I'm sorry I don't have my notes in front of me, she said.

He wrote down the pertinent information on the back of an envelope—the time, the place, the occasion, the duration of his performance (60 minutes including Q & A), and put it down in a prominent place on his dresser top among the other scraps of paper with important notations. He imagined he had a lot to say on the subject—he had been married three times, hadn't he?—but when he sat down in front of his computer to knock out a draft or assemble some notes, his collected wisdom seemed to exhaust itself in half a page.

He blamed his difficulties on the broadness and ambiguity of the topic. What was meant, after all, by "after marriage"? Was it divorce, which had been his original idea, or the dailiness of the marriage itself?

He woke in the middle of the night with the idea of interviewing each of his former wives on what it was like to have been married to him. It would be a way of positioning himself in the talk from the vantage of a person who had gone through the ordeal with him. The idea lost some of its luster in the morning when he remembered that one of his former wives was out of the country and another, still unforgiving, was not likely to give him the time of day.

After some anxious deliberation, he did call G, his most recent ex.

—I'm curious, he said, after asking how she was and not waiting for an answer, what was it like to be married to me.

—Pure hell, she said, laughing.

—You don't really mean that, do you? I know the last year was difficult. What was it like before things went bad?

—The only thing I remember is the last few months and how much I hated you then.

—You don't remember the early years of our marriage being a happy time? We did live together for sixteen years.

—Fifteen years, eight months and three days, she said.

—Did you feel there was a tug of wills between us from the very beginning?

—As a matter of fact, yes. Though we did get by that after awhile.

—We did, didn't we? How did we manage to do that?

—It's not something I've thought about, she said. This is beginning to seem like one of those unsolicited calls you get that pretends to be a survey and then at the end they try to sell you something.

—Come on, he said. What can I possibly be selling? I have nothing to sell.

—It took me 15 years to find that out, she said. He refused to take the bait.

—I've been asked to give a talk on marriage and its aftermath, he said, and I would like to present your side of things as a counterbalance to mine.

—So you do have an ulterior motive for this call, she said. You want me to give you material for your talk. I don't think that's appropriate, do you? You can say, on the authority of one of your former wives, that when it mattered you were not capable of real intimacy, and leave it at that.

—And you were, I suppose? he said, surprised at the belligerence in his voice.

—Oh fuck off, she said.

—I love you too, he said.

And she hung up, not right away, but after a beat or two of indecision. He had the sense, lying down—their conversation had exhausted him—that he had heard whatever it was she had decided not to say.

She was another man's wife, that's all he remembers about their first meeting, not the place or time of day or how attractive she looked or what words they exchanged. He was teaching at a large Midwestern university then, was working on a book of poems. When his officemate was away, she, who he would one day marry, sat, uninvited, at the other desk in his office and read or watched him silently, sphinxlike in her silence. He recognized her somnambulistic presence as a kind of summoning, though he didn't have time to pay attention. Her sadness, if that's what it was, fed into his. She was like some stray cat who had adopted him.

At first her relentless presence burdened him. She had come to him to be looked after, which was his role with women (she knew that right away), but he didn't want the job or didn't want it quite enough to give up whatever else he was tending—his book, his courses, his own unhappy marriage.

If she was not in the room with him, she was always somehow there on the periphery of his vision. He could tell she was annoyed that he paid so little attention to her, but she was not his responsibility even though she acted as if there was some unspecified pact between them.

It gets so, that when she is not there, those days she does not show up, he suffers the rebuke implied by her absence.

On the day of JFK's assassination, she calls him at home for the first time, inviting him to a mourners party at some graduate student's pad. She is crying when she makes the call and pleads with him to come. He says he will try to make it, which she doesn't accept.

–I need you to come, she says.

Does he tell his wife (he doesn't remember exactly) where he's going when he leaves the house that night? Perhaps he asks his wife to come with him and she says to go without her, which is what he ends up doing whichever way it is. Not long after he arrives at the party (he remembers finishing two-thirds of a Rolling Rock and taking the bottle with him), they leave together in his car. He thinks he is driving her home while she appears to believe (she has been drinking steadily for several hours) that they are going off somewhere on an adventure. When he pulls up in front of her house, she rages at him. He may have brought her home but she's not leaving the car, she says, insisting that he take her somewhere else. When he turns off the ignition she punches him in the side with such ferocity that he feels the pain through his heavy jacket as sharply as if he'd been stabbed. They sit silently together for an extended period of time, her head on his shoulder. Eventually she leaves the car and walks a crooked line toward her door. She rings the bell and when no one comes she takes a key from her coat pocket and lets herself in.

This ugly misadventure is the most memorable night of their courtship.

B

2.
B arrived at the Fort Hamilton Armory in Brooklyn for his presentation almost a half hour late, having gotten the time wrong (he had actually sat in the car for 20 minutes, thinking himself early). An impressive crowd of mostly middle-aged women, an array of large purses in their laps, awaited him, almost every seat in the basement auditorium filled. A surly buzz greeted his belated arrival.

The president of the Femmes Club, an imposingly tall woman (the one with the throaty voice who spoke to him on the phone), introduced him to the crowd by reading the bio from the jacket of one of his books, a novel of some 16 years back entitled "A Three-Sided Marriage," and then added with a small rhetorical flourish, –It's been a longstanding policy of our club to bring in speakers of widely divergent and provocative points of view and in this case I believe we have someone with the capacity to get a rise out of even the most even-tempered among us. As is also our policy, you will have opportunity to challenge the speaker with your usually thoughtful and hard-hitting questions after his address. I wish to remind you again that anyone throwing objects from the audience will be asked to leave.

B didn't have to take a reading of the faces in the auditorium to know that he was in hostile territory. He hesitated before beginning, waited for a jolt of inspiration, not daring to look at the inappropriate notes he had written for himself on the coffee-stained cards he had placed on the podium.

–You have me at a disadvantage, he started. I have never given a talk or even a reading in front of a group as large and informed as…(he has momentarily forgotten the name of the club) yours. My expertise on the subject you've assigned me is circumstantial and, I would guess from the standpoint of an outsider, unworthy. I have collaborated with three different women on three failed marriages. I suppose I could try to tell you what went wrong in each case, though my memory of telltale incidents is vague on all but the most recent of my failed liaisons. What is it that Tolstoy says—Leo Tolstoy, the great Russian writer—at the opening of his novel, Anna Karenina, which has also been made into several movies? "Happy families are all alike. Each unhappy family is different in its own way." I quote from unreliable memory. I think that marriages fail because we hold too high an expectation for them. Or that we hold unrealistic romanticized views of our partners when we marry them. And then when disillusion settles in on both sides, as it will, as it must, we feel tricked and deceived, one of us does or both, which makes us, as I don't have to tell you, angry and unhappy. Angry and unhappy leads to bad behavior, leads to going outside the marriage to get (and I'm not speaking only about sex but mostly) what we're not getting at home. Affection, sex, love, companionship. Intimacy. A sense of being desirable. The inability to adjust to the breakdown of illusion and the loss of passion is what brings marriages to grief and irreparable disrepair or allows them to survive in pained, unhappy ways. And then, at least in my case, we start all over again and the pattern reasserts itself. In answer to the question: After Marriage, What?, I would say 1. Disappointment 2. Anger 3. Children 4. Betrayal and 5. Divorce, though not necessarily in that order. What keeps us reading on is that the particulars tend to be different with each new partnership.

He has said all of the above almost without stopping to breathe and now he collects himself and looks out at the audience. They seem less antagonistic than before, though perhaps that is because several have nodded off and some others, whose eyes are open, have glazed looks.

—Maybe I should have started by telling you something about myself, he continues. I confess when I arrived here I had no idea how to approach the topic. The reason that many of my novels present alternate scenarios to the same event is not because I am a experimental writer, whatever that is, but because I tend to believe that there are always other possibilities in a narrative or a life that might be explored. For example instead of regaling you with my ideas about marriage—the wisdom gained from unhappy experience—I might have described for you some of my adventures in the marriage trade and let you draw your own conclusions. I matured late and my social skills as a teenager with the opposite sex ran the gamut from pathetic to embarrassing. In fact, I was technically a virgin until I was almost 19 and not for want of trying. I was in love with my first girlfriend but we broke up after going together in college for three years, which I've regretted to this day. My first marriage lasted nine months, at which point my child bride went home to her mother and never returned. I had an interlude in the army between my first wife and my second, who I met on leave after basic training. A noisy affair with the woman who would become my third wife was instrumental in wrecking my second marriage, which is to say I left wife 2 for wife 3. You have every reason to wonder, as I do sometimes myself, why I expected to be happier with wife 3 than I had been with wife 2. Well, for one, I had already lived with wife 2 for seven plus years and we had by that time thoroughly trashed what had once been an intimate friendship, avoiding each other programatically, rarely talking, almost never making love. Also, I barely knew wife 3, beyond our illicit once-a-week sexual encounters, so getting together with her represented a fresh start, a chance to prove I could make a good life with another person. Wife 2 already knew all my faults and then some, and she was a woman with small tolerance for imperfection. Wife 3, before we were married at least, tended to see me in the most generous light, which gave me renewed sense of pleasure in myself. So what else could I do but divorce wife 2 and move in with the woman whose love I shared, whose love sustained me. I mean, almost anyone in my situation who had an open mind would have done the same. And still, I confess this openly, I was and I am opposed to divorce, I was and I am opposed to adultery, I believed and believe in the sanctity and permanence of marriage. Does that make any sense? I was in love with wife 3, who aside from being a little crazy, seemed almost perfect to me. Love was my excuse for moving on. A loveless marriage is no marriage at all, I told myself. I had to take on faith that there was a time in the distant past, long gone and long forgotten, when I loved wife 2, and even as I acknowledged the probability, I didn't believe it, couldn't. Wife 3 was the woman I was meant to spend the rest of my life alongside so in a sense you see it was my first real marriage. You see I had to go through the disappointment and grief of two marriages that didn't count to get to the one I was meant to have. I don't believe I thought consciously about my choices in the terms I just offered you, but it stands to reason that those were my reasons. Hey, I was following the dictates of my heart. How could anyone find fault with that? So after 16 years when my third wife dumped me for another, the failure of this marriage was all the more bitter. I had to reevalue my sense of self. If I was this monogamous person, which was how I continued to see myself, how come I had been married and divorced three times by the time I was 47? Actually, I thought my third marriage had been going fairly well until my wife told me she preferred someone else. I could understand that in the abstract. Hadn't I left wife 2 because I also preferred someone else? So I took wife 3's disaffection as a kind of poetic justice. I had behaved badly to wife 2 so I got paid back in kind by wife 3. Fair enough. Still I was heartbroken for a few years, even after I moved in with another woman and another woman after that, old patterns reasserting themselves in accelerated time. My post-marital liaisons were merely a variation on the themes already deconstructed so there is no need to describe them for you here. Suffice to say, I am living alone these days, though still dating the last of the women I lived with briefly, still playing the same old game. V and I are probably better friends since we stopped living together, which is another issue that might be explored. A certain residual bitterness remains, which flames out disconcertingly from time to time. We both of us rage over the failure of our once promising relationship, and point fingers and mourn our losses.

B was about to say something about how he felt toward women as a group, as people you live with intimately and then no longer live with, when he noticed that the imposingly tall gray-haired woman who had introduced him was pointing at her watch.

—Why don't I stop here? B said, and allow whatever else I might have to say to come out in answer to your questions.

Now his hostess was shaking her head as to suggest that he had misread her original signal. Still, there was a hand raised in the back row and B felt obliged to recognize the questioner. It was a youngish woman, someone in her forties perhaps, one of the youngest there.

—What would be your advice to a young person considering marriage in today's world?

—I don't feel I've earned the right to give advice, B said.

—Would you discourage such a person? the woman asked.

—I think people should be free to make their own mistakes, he said.

—That's certainly discouraging, she said, and sat down.

For a while there were no hands raised as B let his glance move up and down the room, picking up sympathetic responses here and there, a wan smile, an encouraging nod. In the next moment, five or six hands were up vying for his attention. He pointed to a small grandmotherly white-haired woman in the third row. —Me? she asked, rising partially from her seat. He nodded yes. She looked around her, still apparently not sure that she was the one he meant.

—I was not born in this country, she said, so excuse me if I don't get what all the fuss is about. You say you've been married three times. Is that what you said—three? I think I must be missing something. Am I supposed to be impressed? I was married five times myself and that was in the old days when things were different. And if the truth be known, I didn't see the point of it much of the time even then. I can't say I remember enjoying my obligations all that much. My sister, Manuela, was the one who enjoyed sex. So I ask you, what's the fuss? Tell me and I'll know.

—I've often asked myself that same question, B said.

—So?

—I never came up with an answer I trusted, B said....Next question.

—Answer her, someone shouted from the audience. A few other women stamped their feet in chorus. Answer her. Answer her.

The room began to vibrate and B, who could think of nothing to say, struggled to come up with something that would pacify the crowd. —The fuss is, B said, the fuss is that women are so damned attractive to us that we continue to pursue them even when we know that humiliation and disaster beckons. Perhaps it works the other way around as well. You tell me.

He recognized a short-haired mousy woman with glasses in the first row, waving her hand furiously at him. —So what you're saying is that women marry men only to destroy them in the end. Is that your point?

—No, he said, it's not. I have the highest respect for women's intentions in and out of marriage. That remark drew some hisses from the crowd and as a follow-up a smattering of applause. It consoled him that there were still a few people in the audience on his side.

It went on this way for awhile, people asking confrontational questions and B sidestepping them as best he knew how, wanting not to offend or not to offend too much. He was getting increasingly concerned about getting out of the armory after the Q and A period was finally over. He glanced at his watch and noted that more than an hour had passed since the first question had been asked.

—I've enjoyed this friendly exchange of ideas with you, he said, hoping to bring the proceedings to an end with a summation. I've learned so much from you today. Perhaps if we had this meeting years back, I might have avoided the various mistakes I made over the years in my relationships with women.

—Blow it out your ass, a large woman near the back yelled.

—Where is this leading? someone else shouted out.

—You haven't listened to a fucking word we've said, from still another.

—As I was saying, B said, I think it's possible for men and women to live together...

—Get him out of here, from two or three at once.

—...happily for short periods of time.

—We don't want to live with you, another said, happily or unhappily. We just want you to go away. Don't you get it?

—I appreciate your honesty, B said, and your directness of approach. When someone says to me the kind of things you've been saying, I feel I've been taken seriously. At this point an unidentified flying object, a small plastic hairbrush perhaps, whipped by his left ear and B flinched, then raised his arms in mock surrender. A tomato followed, propelled by cheers and laughter, splattering at his feet.

—Please, he heard his hostess, the organization's president, call from somewhere behind him, this man is a guest in your house. An orange or tangerine scaled his shoulder in a loopy arc.

—Is that the best you can do? he shouted at them. Momentarily, he was pelted with fruit, oranges, apples and tomatoes launched from the auditorium, the missiles inaccurately thrown for the most part, though B thought it wise to duck down behind the podium to avoid the accidental hit.

When the flight of fruit subsided, the president of the Femmes Club came forward to make her concluding remarks. —They are an excitable crowd, she said to B, who exchanged places with her, taking the seat somewhat to the right and behind the podium she had previously occupied. He was still somewhat shaken—he had never had a crowd respond to him as violently as this one had. No one, said unreliable memory, had ever thrown fruit at him before with intent to harm.

—We will meet again in four weeks, his hostess told the crowd, when we'll address the topic, "Who's on Top, What's on Bottom?"

Taking B aside, she suggested in a whisper that he wait for the audience to clear out before he made his exit. Then she handed him an envelope which B put in the breast pocket of his jacket. —It's the best we can do, she said, the context for the moment difficult to pin down.

As the audience stood up to leave, he noticed that his second wife or a woman who bore her an uncanny resemblance was among the exiting crowd. That her back was to him made it difficult for him to make a positive identification. He was about to call out to her when his hostess took his arm and led him out the back door into the Weapons Room, walls lined with carbines and M-1's locked away in windowed cases.

—This is our Green Room, she told him, introducing herself as Gladys Fleur.

B found himself moved to gratitude by her unlooked for civility.

Gladys came up with a dusty bottle of Scotch that had been on one of the counters and offered him a drink, which he refused and then accepted.

—I think it's a good idea to let the crowd disperse before you leave the building, she said. Not that I expect the worst to happen but there's a saying that I tend to trust, which is "Better safe than sorry."

B looked at his watch. —I appreciate your concern, he said,

but I'm expected somewhere.

He took a few sips of his drink, then put the glass down and held out his hand.

—It's not personal, she said, ignoring his gesture. It's just that I'm opposed to violence no matter the justice of the cause. If you're ready to leave, I'll show you out.

3.

B wondered as he followed his guide down a succession of unlit corridors how this experience, still unconcluded, might be made into a fiction. It might be an interesting irony if his antihero ended up marrying the head of the militant feminist group his well-meaning talk had clumsily offended. It might be as they walked in the darkening corridors to the back exit, they locked hands so as not to get separated. The hand-holding, not initially meant as an intimacy, might make B aware of Gladys' attractiveness as a woman, the sweetness and warmth of her repressed nature. And she in turn might find herself drawn to B despite her predilection to perceive him as the enemy. He might offer to take her to dinner that night as she lets him out the door as a repayment for her kindness. Gladys says thank you no, it's out of the question, she'd prefer never to see him again, but he continues to insist until he wears her down. Over dinner they discover that they have more things in common than they have any right to suppose. Gladys is also a poet or has been and paints on weekends and is an obsessive moviegoer, passionate about some of the same films as B.

If she sees him again, she says—this, after they have spectacular sex for the first time—it will have to be done in secrecy, her friends and constituency would view a relationship between them as totally unacceptable. And so on and so until it reaches a point where the undercover aspect of the relationship as if they were a two-person terrorist cell has become more nuisance than guilty pleasure and B asks her to move in with him. She says no, not yet, soon, sometime, when I'm ready, when we're both ready, isn't it good enough the way it is, let's take a trip to Europe first, to Paris or to one of the hill towns in Italy, as soon as we both can get away and see how we track together, to which B accedes though not without trepidation since he has been in this very place in several relationships before with the same manic hopefulness or less or more and he begins to feel—this after she tells him she loves him—an impingement in his chest, an abridgement in his range of motion even among the beauties of Umbria or wherever it is they've decided to go, an airlessness without respite even while out of doors, and he knows it's no longer working, as she must too, but the desire to make things work won't let them acknowledge this full-blown disaster either privately or to each other and they agree to marry on their return to the states however deplorable this marriage might seem to friends and family on both sides and to themselves, it will be a litmus test to see who remains in their good graces.

That's the story he imagines he will someday write about the experience at the Fort Hamilton Armory as a guest speaker before the Femmes Club, the imagining taking place as he skulks along behind his hostess to an exit that will place him outside the building far from the angry and potentially dangerous crowd. When they reach the door, she says —Let me go first to make sure it's all clear. As she is opening the door, he squeezes her arm as a gesture of gratitude and she turns toward him, letting the door swing shut, panic in her gray eyes as she wraps her arms around him and they hug and nuzzle in a kind of hungry, somewhat desperate way, holding each other for a moment that extends itself, a moment that seems to go on so long that he begins to feel his life slipping away as he idles in her embrace. And then: she slaps his face, the blow staggering him. When he looks at her, an unblinking rage stares back. There is nothing to be said, nothing to do but leave the armory without further delay.

When B steps outside, the streets are empty as if the world had stopped its business in his absence. An icy wind flies in his face. He puts up the collar of his coat, and hurries in what feels to him like slow-motion—the wind resisting his need to be where he's not—toward his parked car. Then, playing back the immediate past in his head, he is overtaken by an unaccountable, almost perverse joy.

He discovers himself smiling. He smiles.

X. THE HISTORY OF ELEGANCE

1.
There is no history of elegance, says V, the woman in the green suede coat, to B who has his hand on her arm. She is responding to a sign that appears in purple lights in the window of a Madison Avenue men's shop.

It is not an issue that interested B before this moment, though he feels obliged to take a stand. The History of Elegance is the story of my life, he says.

The woman laughs; B has a history of being amusing while seeming to be serious, a history of saying the most incongruous thing that comes to mind. It sounds like a very short story in your case, she says.

B turns away, studies the passing scene, straightens his tie. He wonders at the meaning of her remark, feels himself misunderstood.

The woman slaps her forehead. I suppose I'm always missing the point, she says.

Is she being just a little ironic? he wonders. They walk along Madison Ave., their mutual reality glancing off the elegant displays in the windows of the boutiques they pass.

I never know when you're being serious, she says. I wonder sometimes if you know.

If I know what?

Forget it, she says. You're absolutely impossible.

He would like to tell her the story of The History of Elegance, though he suspects it would only increase her misunderstanding of him.

My feet are beginning to hurt, she says.

I don't know where to begin, B tells her. It's a recurrent problem of mine, how to begin. I try to work my way into it, come to my subject from some undisclosed angle. What happens is, I never get to what I perceive as the real story. The preliminaries—the way into the story—become the story itself.

How interesting, she says. When I was married to George—I never told anyone this before—this man I knew in a roundabout way asked me if I would go to Italy with him. Just like that. We were having lunch—he had invited me to lunch—and he said, I'm going to Italy in ten days and I'd like you to come with me.

How long was he going for? B asks, not yet engaged by her story.

For the rest of his life as far as he knew, she says. His firm was sending him to Rome. It wasn't for a weekend or something like that. I never would have gone off with him for a weekend.

I never heard this story before, he says. They pass a bookstore and out of the corner of his eye, he thinks he sees a copy of his most recent novel. Closer inspection disabuses him of the notion. It is something with a similar title and a much too similar cover design.

I think I told you some of this, she says. No? He was a really elegant man—I mean, really elegant. His clothes fit him like a second skin. When he asked I said I couldn't possibly. There was my daughter to consider. He said it was perfectly all right if I brought her along, then I said I needed some time to think about it. I was stalling because I didn't know how to refuse him gracefully. There was no way I could leave my husband and child at that time. How could I?

Do you mind if we go into the bookstore for a few minutes? he says. I want to see if they have my book on the shelf.

They spend no more than thirty seconds in the bookstore then leave. It is how long it takes to discover that there is no copy of his book on the shelf.

I spent the next two days thinking about his offer, she says. The more I thought about it, the more I thought Why not? What was there to stop me?

I should have asked them if it's on reorder, B says. I'm always embarrassed to ask about my own book.

Do you want me to ask them whether your book is on order, she says. Really, I don't mind.

It doesn't matter, he says. Did you go off with this man who wore a vest even in the bathtub?

I never said he wore a vest in the bathtub, she says. Are you being funny, darling? I mean really he had a natural elegance, and he had very good clothes. Almost everything he wore looked as though it had been made expressly for him.

I dislike this man already, he says.

You would have liked him if you knew him, she says. Most men liked him. Even George liked him. Do you want to hear the rest of this or not?

They had passed the Whitney Museum, walking north on Madison Ave. B was struck by a memory concerning the museum, or an intuition of a memory, that refused to come into focus. It had something to do with his father who did a painting the Whitney owned that was almost never on display.

I don't like men whose clothes fit them too well, he says. I know you didn't go off with him. Your story has no real suspense.

But I did, she says. Why are you so sure I didn't go? You're so arrogant. Three days after he asked me, I told George that I was leaving him to go to Italy. George was crushed. I felt terrible about it.

I can understand that, he says. Would you like to take in the minimalist show at the Whitney? What do you say, babe?

I've already seen it, she says. I was there last week. I don't remember what day, Thursday or Friday.

Where was I?

Wherever you were, she says. If you really want to go, I'll go again.

That's all right, he says, but they turn around and walk the block and a half back to the museum.

Once I told my husband I was leaving, she says, I realized I had put myself in a really precarious position. He was hurt, I could tell, but he was not about to plead with me to stay. He did insist, however, that Carolyn be allowed to finish the term at her school. I insisted on taking her right away. I said the school didn't matter. Besides, I was the one who took care of her, not George. I was the one who got her meals and bought her clothes and put her to bed at night. She was just six years old at the time. She needed her mother.

B acknowledges her remarks with a nod. He is an indifferent listener, but he imagines someday he'll improve his skills. They are in front of the Whitney now, seemingly undecided on what to do next. B takes the woman's arm. We don't have to stay very long, he says. The woman shakes her head but nevertheless follows him inside. He buys tickets for both of them, though the woman says she'd rather wait for him in the lobby.

I want to hear the rest of your story about Italy, he says.

The woman laughs. I don't think you've been listening very hard, she says. Anyway when I look at paintings all my senses are occupied. She says this in a declamatory voice.

It is the kind of remark, B thinks, that invites applause. He announces in an equally assertive voice that there are certain shows he can see with his eyes at half mast, and that this may be one of them. A minimalist show requires a minimalist response.

Sometimes I think you confuse cynicism with wit, she says. I'll wait for you out here. I have a book in my purse I can read.

Why don't we just go, B says, catching his reflection in a mirror sculpture in a far corner of the lobby. His cast off image has a kind of dignity that surprises him.

Oh go see the show, she says. You might even like it. At your pace you'll be in and out in under ten minutes.

B leaves the museum and the woman trails after him.

After walking a block and a half in silence, he says, Did you go to Italy or didn't you?

I told you I went, she says. You seem not to want to believe it. Once I told George I was leaving, I virtually had to go whether I wanted to or not. Do you understand that?

How is it I never knew you lived in Italy? he asks. I've known you for almost five years.

His question seems to annoy her and she quickens her pace,

walks on ahead. I don't think you listen when I talk, she says when he catches up. I'm sure I mentioned something of this to you.

I would have remembered, he says. I hear most of what you say.

Most of, she says. From now on when I tell you something I'm going to test you on it afterwards.

Let's go into the park, he says. Is that all right?

Whatever you want to do, she says.

They cross Madison against the light, find themselves facing the Metropolitan Museum as they move toward the park.

I wish you weren't so acquiescent, he says.

That's an odd complaint, she says. Would you like it better if I were difficult?

You are difficult, he says.

I don't know if you're joking or not, she says. How am I difficult? I'd like to know what you think is difficult about me.

The most difficult thing about you, he says, looking behind them as if he sensed they were being followed, is the difficulty I have putting what's difficult about you into words.

So you're joking, she says. I don't like it that you joke about everything. I really don't.

I'm joking and you're also difficult, he says. The two don't exclude one another. Why did you leave your family and go off to Italy with that fop?

I can't believe you said that, she says. If I thought you were going to judge me, I wouldn't have told you any of this....I went off with him because I thought I was in love with him. I don't think you want to hear any of this.

I'm trying to understand you, he says. Did you believe you were in love with him before he asked you to go with him?

They go around the museum into the park, the woman a half step ahead of B, walking at an unusually quick pace.

I'm not saying any more, she says in a sulky voice. You don't want to hear any more of this story.

B puts his arm around her waist. I want to hear the rest of the story, he says. If you won't tell it to me, I'll tell the story for you.

You'll get nothing more from me, she says. Not a word.

B puts his hand over his eyes, imagines the elegant man and the beautiful younger woman waiting at the airport for their flight to Rome, which is not yet available for boarding. Waiting for their plane, B says, the woman is full of enthusiasm for the prospect of her new life, doesn't allow herself to be in touch with whatever feelings of regret exist under the surface of her exuberant manner. She chatters, is mildly hysterical. The elegant man, whose manner is at once comforting and distant, tells her that if she wants to change her mind, the option remains open to her. She is under no pressure to do anything she doesn't want to do. The woman says that she has made her decision and it is irrevocable.

Are you absolutely sure? her host asks. He repeats the question again when they arrive in Rome.

The first two days are the hardest for her, the period of most intense regret. She reads books, practices her Italian, sleeps fifteen hours a day. What am I doing here? she asks herself as she stares out the window of her apartment at the unfamiliar streets. Her companion is busy setting up his office, seeing people. A month passes, and she readies herself for her daughter's arrival. A friend of hers is accompanying Caroline on her flight to Rome in five days. Everything is arranged, or everything seems to be arranged.

She gets a call in the middle of the night from her friend in New York. Her husband has decided at the last minute not to let the daughter come. In a fury the woman calls her husband and demands to know what's going on. I've decided not to let Caroline go, the husband says. I've talked to my lawyer and he says I'm perfectly within my rights. His tone is icy. The woman is devastated, hangs up on him in frustration, calls back, reminds him of his promise to send Caroline after she finished school, reminds him of what's best for their daughter. Her husband is unmoved by her appeal.

The woman says, The reason I left you is because I sensed you were capable of this kind of treachery. You have no character. It is her parting shot, her acknowledgment of defeat.

The next step has a certain inevitability. She has to go back to the states to recover her daughter. Still, she delays her trip, delays telling her companion of her decision, delays until her anxiety threatens to implode her into fragments.

2.
The woman looks at her watch, says, I really have to go in a few minutes.

You never said anything about going anywhere, B says. I thought we'd have dinner together.

I have another appointment, she says.

I'll cancel my appointment if you cancel yours, he says.

They are in the park behind the museum, walking so slowly they seem to be standing still.

I know you're not being serious, she says. Am I right?

I have no other appointment, he says, but if I had one, I would have canceled it to have dinner with you.

She thinks about it, seems to be thinking about the implication of his remark. I like that you would have broken your date for me, she says.

I'm not going to ask you to break your date for me, he says. He looks at his watch, makes a point of it. I always end up feeling angry at you. Why is that?

That's not a question I can answer for you, she says. If you're suggesting it's my fault, you're way off base. I have no idea why you're angry at me.

He looks at her, shakes his head, walks off in no particular direction.

Don't do this, she calls after him.

B walks about ten steps, then stops and turns around. He is not surprised to see the woman coming after him.

You're impossible, she says. That's why there's never been any hope for us. They walk for a while with their arms around each other.

What do you want me to do? she asks him.

I want you to do what you want to do, he says. You're a free person.

Whatever that means, she says. If I'm a free person, whatever,

I'm going to keep my appointment. I don't know what else you expect.

He laughs. I haven't had an expectation in years, he says. Well, I'll see you around. He turns to go.

I'll walk with you to your car, she says. Are you angry at me? You have no reason to be angry.

He walks quickly with his head thrust forward, as if he were countering some unseen force that would otherwise stop him in his tracks, and the woman asks him, her hand on his arm, to slow down please.

I didn't even know you were with me, he says, slowing down but not so it mattered.

Maybe we ought to say good-bye here, she says, a half-step behind, trying to keep up. You're behaving in a childish manner.

Good-bye, he says.

B slows down and they walk together in a desultory way to his car, neither quite acknowledging the other.

Good-bye, he says again, not looking at her.

Which direction are you going? she asks. Could you drop me somewhere?

I'm going downtown, he says, as if that settled the matter.

She nods to herself in answer to some unspoken thought.

I have some errands to run in the Village. Is that out of your way?

He looks off into the distance. I'll take you to the Village, he says without enthusiasm.

B opens the passenger door of the car for her.

On second thought, she says, maybe I'd better not. I really don't have that much time.

He is holding the door open for her when she says that and he closes it in slow motion.

I'm going to have to pass, she says. I'm sorry. Thanks for the offer.

He doesn't say anything, offers no indication of his feelings one way or another, goes around to the other side and gets into the car.

She is saying something to him and he has to unroll his window to hear her.

I didn't stay in Rome at all, she says. I went back to New York on the next plane.

B nods, he knows what it is to sacrifice one desire for another, starts up the car, waves to the woman, who seems to be waiting for him to pull away before she leaves. Suddenly the woman walks briskly off in no particular direction. The car doesn't move; B lingers, seems to be waiting for something to happen, the car idling. As she reaches the corner, the woman turns to look back, which at once surprises B and is what he has anticipated happening. She can't give him up, he tells himself, perhaps projecting his own unadmitted feelings on to her.

Since B is imagining the event, you might think the woman would experience a change of heart and turn around and run toward him, hoping to reach his car before he left the scene. It might even happen in tricked-up slow motion as in the fade out of a movie. Instead, the woman descends the subway steps and vanishes temporarily from our concern.

XI. AN ANNOTATED HISTORY OF THE PAST

1.
Since retirement, a kind of authorized idleness, I read the obits every morning with my breakfast coffee. The death report has replaced the sports section in my life as the news of first urgency. I don't know what I hope to find, whose death, whose life, whose unlikely story. It may only be that I'm confirming my own de facto survival by not discovering my name among the recent departed.

I took early retirement on the advice of Dr. Goodenuv, an old friend of the family, himself partially retired, in order to relieve stress which does no one any good. The new stress-free regimen in my life, my days of idleness and ease, has been dispiriting so far. I feel like an impostor hanging out at home all day, cultivating my inner garden, which at the moment is mired in weeds. A former girlfriend says I need to have sex more often, though has also made it clear that she is not offering her participation along with the advice.

Routine tends to establish itself among those of us who need the trappings of order. I tend to write for little more than an hour each morning, then talk on the phone until it is time for lunch. The afternoons are given over to checking out the movies on TV—I have seven (count them) commercial-free movie channels—followed by the after-lunch walk and the after-walk nap.

After my nap, I tend to read the sports section to see what's shaking in the world of fantasy. When I feel up to it, I reread a novel by Charles Dickens or Henry James or Thomas Hardy. My memory is bad enough that each rereading seems a maiden voyage.

Besides, it relieves anxiety to sense the outcome in advance.

It is still morning on this particular day. I am browsing through the obits while nursing my second cup of caffeine-free coffee. And bam! I have a discomforting, unsought, privileged moment. I find what I have apparently been looking for. Up to this point, I have been merely a browser in the neighborhood of grief. In small print at the bottom of the page it reads: Dolores Kovaleski(néeWinespot), actress, dead of cancer at 61. Played the eccentric nurse Hanna in the long-running soap, "The Lights of Our Days." Survived by estranged husband Fred and two divorced daughters, Deborah and Deidre.

Didi Winespot had been my first serious girlfriend, though I haven't actually thought about her in ages. She had loved me, says tattered evidence of memory. I had loved her too but less unequivocally. I was unformed when I knew her. My feelings for her had been tempered by ambivalence and a free-floating sense of unworthiness. But hasn't that always been my story?

I was at Columbia, she was at Barnard. Having nothing better to do with my evening, I had gone to this freshman mixer, not usually my kind of thing, was sampling the punch when she came up behind me and said, —Hi there, as if we shared some intimate history. She was familiar looking, though I couldn't remember having met her before. At 18, I generally avoided women who put me at a disadvantage.

—Do we know each other? I asked her.

—Not until you tell me your name, she said.

I liked her style, though it also made me uncomfortable.

When I asked her to dance, she said she had hoped when she came up to me that I was someone who, like herself, didn't dance. Again she had me at a disadvantage. —I don't dance either, I said. I just go through the motions.

—Well, in that case, she said, I suppose I will accept your invitation.

It may have been that she didn't dance (as a rule), but it wasn't because she couldn't. She was better than good, which was what I thought of telling her and did in my understated (unstated) way.

—Why did you say you couldn't dance? I asked after the music had stopped.

She corrected my misassumption. –What I said was that I didn't dance, she said.

I spent the rest of the evening in her company, which included taking her home in my father's car. At some point, stuck at a red light, I wondered what she would do if I kissed her but I let the thought, a characteristic failing of mine, suffice for the act. I also didn't get to kiss her goodnight when I dropped her off and I held her accountable for my reticence.

When we crossed paths on campus for the next week or so, I looked the other way, embarrassed at how ineptly I had handled myself in her company. Then one day, I saw her coming toward me on the steps of Loeb Hall and there was no avoiding her. So I opened my arms to her as a grandiose gesture parodying itself and she, no stranger to play, accepted her role in my improvised charade. We hugged like some movie idea of lovers meeting again after an extended period of enforced absence. I lifted her off her feet and swung her about. I was the first to let go.

–I've been meaning to call you, I lied.

She had an extra ticket for the City Center ballet for tomorrow night, she said. Was that something that interested me?

It wasn't particularly, which is to say I didn't know if it did or not. I had never even so much as entertained the possibility before. –Yeah, I said, sure. I considered asking what was playing, but decided it was probably not the appropriate question.

Another couple accompanied us, Didi's older sister and her fiancé. They all were so knowledgable about the dancers, even the sister's smug lawyer boyfriend, that except for a few sassy remarks, I took refuge in silence. I knew myself out of my depth in this company on this occasion and so disguised my resentment by playing the secretly superior outsider.

–You're so quiet, she whispered to me in the back of the boyfriend's car on the return drive to her dorm, punctuating the remark with a poke in my side. Tell me what you're thinking.

If one couldn't keep one's thoughts secret, what hope was there for the shy dissembler? As a way of changing the subject, I took her hand and kissed the palm. I felt aggressive and momentarily in charge.

—If you don't mean it, don't do it, she said sulkily.

We were both silent until they dropped us in front of the Barnard dorms.

—You don't have to walk me to the door, she said.

—What if I want to, I said belligerently. My own voice surprised me. It was the first words I had heard myself speak since we left the theater.

She laughed nervously. —Are you trying to be absurd? she asked. If so, you're succeeding remarkably.

—Let's walk around the block, I said. I don't want us to separate like this.

She took my arm and we walked slowly down the street. At the corner, we stopped to kiss. —I don't want to like you too much, she said when we came apart. You're an angry person and angry persons are not to be trusted.

I didn't hesitate for even a moment of circumspection but issued a blanket denial of her charge. At 18 (a young 18 at that), I was prepared at any given moment to deny any aspersions against my character, that unfamiliar acquaintance that followed me everywhere.

—Do you consider yourself trustworthy? she asked, looking directly at me.

I dealt with the question by deferring my answer, by shrugging my shoulders, by pretending to myself it had not been asked. We turned around and walked back toward her building, our truce on fragile ground.

—I know it's an unfair question, she said, but those are the most fun to ask. Well, are you or aren't you?

—I think we need to get to know each other better, I said, before either of us can answer that question.

—Oh, she said. And what if that never happens?

After she opened the door with her key, she turned back to let me kiss her, but when I dawdled, thanking her dutifully for the ballet, announcing what a good time I had, which clearly she didn't believe, she said, —Goodnight, and closed the door virtually in my face with decisive impatience.

Her abrupt dismissal troubled me and I called the next evening to sound her out. What had I done to offend? She seemed so pleased to hear from me, so openly and undisguisedly pleased, that it made me think I had misread the gesture of her seemingly dismissive goodbye. We made a date for the following Saturday night, and after that we became an item on campus. For the next three years, hardly a day went by when we didn't share each other's time.

She critiqued my poems with that rare combination of unsparing honesty and good will for which one is always, if grudgingly, indebted, and I in turn helped her learn her lines for the various plays she performed in. There was Laura in "The Glass Menagerie," as I recall, and Tracy in "The Philadelphia Story," and The Girl in "Outpost of Despair," a blank verse play written by me of which there are, with good reason, no surviving copies.

Though we kept separate rooms—there were no coed dorms in those days—we spent so much time together people referred to us as "the Siamese twins."

And then, approximately three years after she had asked the question, my errant behavior answered it. Yes, I was not trustworthy. I had been a time bomb of untrustworthiness set for some vulnerable moment in the distant future. I tended to be a little jealous of the guys who played love scenes with Didi on stage. It wasn't hard for me to imagine that she might prefer one of them to me, or prefer the character one of them was playing to the character I played in real life. When Didi acted, she tended to inhabit the role she was performing (sometimes offstage as well) for the duration of the play. I thought that she went too far in that regard, that such identification with an imaginary character threatened to blur the boundaries between real self and fantasy. It was one of the things we argued goodnaturedly about. We had a habit of teasing each other over inconsequential faults.

Sometimes I wanted to do things that excluded Didi but I rarely did because I felt vulnerable when it was the other way around, when she was the one requesting time apart. I took such requests as a token of worse to come. Having this long term desirable girlfriend should have made me more confident and it did to some extent but it also intensified my insecurities. She was so important in my life, so integral, I couldn't imagine how I would handle her loss, which I sensed was inevitable.

So it was necessary to wean myself of my need for her, a task that at first seemed unimaginable. Nothing is unimaginable of course once it's been imagined. I worked at conceiving the advantages of being unencumbered. The obvious one was that, unattached, I could get together guiltlessly with other attractive girls that were off-limits to me in my present situation. Off-limits, unless I was willing to betray Didi's trust. There was this sexy girl, Elaine, who flirted with me in my Seventeenth Century English Drama Exclusive of Shakespeare class, who occupied space in my fantasies. I deceived myself with rationalizations. A writer feeds off experience. My being with Elaine wouldn't hurt Didi if she didn't know about it. Whatever was between Didi and me (love, I assumed) would survive a one-time-only transgression. And if it didn't, then just maybe the bonds between us were less significant than I had allowed myself to believe.

So I dated Elaine (her last name eludes memory) and made up some improbable tale for Didi about some late paper I needed to stay up all night to finish.

The date was predictably a flop. I had no talent for deception or had too much talent for it to proceed without being undermined by guilt. Unrehearsed in my new role, I was uncharacteristically stiff and distant with this unfamiliar partner. Elaine did her best to put me at ease and we ended the evening fooling around uncomfortably in the front seat of her car.

In the morning, Didi called to ask how my paper was coming and I admitted that progress had been negligible. She commiserated and that was it.

Two weeks later I dropped over to her room unannounced and discovered one of the younger teachers in the English Department sitting next to her on the couch. –You should have called first, she said, seemingly unperturbed at my discovery.

–I was just getting ready to go, the English teacher said, and in short order I was alone with Didi and anxiously unready to take on an explanation of this awkward discovery.

I waited, hand on hip, censorious look on my face. I was

prepared for anything except her refusal to explain herself.

—Probably nothing would have happened, she said. It was not an apology. It was certainly not an explanation.

Her poise provoked me. —What was supposed to happen? I asked.

—If this is going to be a fight, she said, why don't we wait until the morning when we both have more energy?

—I want to know what he was doing in your room, I said.

Didi made a face, shook her head at me. —I'd like you to leave, she said in a sad voice. Get out of here, will you please?

Off-balance, defeated, I felt the need to reclaim whatever power I had in whatever hackneyed fashion I could.

—If I leave like this, I said, it's over between us.

—That's not what I want, she said. You know it's not.

My momentum took me out the door.

In the morning I was full of unaccountable energy and I occupied myself in the hour before my classes by attending to chores I had been putting off indefinitely. I actually straightened up my room, which had been a kind of stage set for romantic disorder, and emptied the overflowing waste basket. I vowed to myself, a pact with my own devil as it turned out, that I would not call her no matter what. However, when she didn't call at the time we usually talked, it registered as a betrayal. It was something else in the balance to hold against her.

We had a class together the next day and I decided to stay away rather than go through the awkwardness of meeting and avoiding my other self.

The following day we crossed paths on Morningside Drive and nodded to each other in ambiguous acknowledgment. After that, I attended the Existential Philosophy class we shared, though changed my seat to the other side of the room.

Another week passed without so much as an exchange of a word between us. A sense of being unforgivable kept me going in my blindly determined path.

One day Elaine called and said she heard I had broken up with Didi and that she hoped I was okay.

—Is that right? I said. Where did you hear that?

—It's all around, she said. Didi has told her friends that it's over. Is that not your view of it?

I conceded that if Didi thought it was over, it would be idle for me to think otherwise.

Elaine wondered if I was in the mood for company and I conceded that I was, more or less, pleased at her taking the burden of decision out of my hands. This time I cooperated in my seduction. I didn't think of Didi while we fucked, made a point of not thinking of her, which made her a kind of invisible third party in our collaborative betrayal. Seeing Elaine made it easier for me not to suffer Didi's loss, so I stayed with the relationship even after my pleasure in it had faded to nothing.

It was Didi finally who called to invite me to a play she was performing in and to say, in passing, that she was sorry things had ended so abruptly between us. The call made me aware of missing her, but I was still angry too, up to my ears in unacknowledged pain and empty pride. I continued to feel obscurely betrayed. I went to watch Didi play Julie in Strindberg's "Miss Julie" with Elaine at my side. We went backstage afterward, Elaine attached to my arm, to make the appropriate noises over Didi's performance.

When Elaine's head was turned, Didi mouthed the words, —Call me.

Her request pleased me and I did call the next morning but she was out when I called or she didn't pick up. Things might have been different had she been there. Her unavailability fueled my anger, and I made a decision not to call again. If Didi wanted to talk to me, wanted to see me again, continued to love me, the next move was hers.

So pride or stubbornness, perhaps on her part too, kept us apart during our senior year. We were at the same parties on occasion each with different dates and had nodded to one another across a crowded room. We avoided conversation as if some unspoken danger lurked in the touch of our voices.

One night, after such a party, the phone rang when I was already in bed. At first I thought not to answer, assuming a wrong number, but when it kept on ringing I leapt out of bed and grabbed the receiver. After I said hello, after some barely audible breathing on the other end, my caller hung up. I knew who was calling (I thought) and sat up in bed for another hour wondering what to do about it, deciding after a while that there was nothing to be done.

I didn't talk to her again until after the graduation ceremony, at which time I shouldered my way through the disorderly crowd hoping to find her alone. When I caught up with her I didn't know what to say so improvised a few banalities about how important her friendship had been to me. Didi made a sassy remark in return then turned around to leave, then turned back to face me again. —Just who the hell do you think you are? she said in the voice of outrage. Her hand was shaking and I was aware of her pressing it to her side to disguise the fact. (I remember it as if it happened only hours ago.) Her anger confused me, made me want to defend myself (from what I didn't know), made me want to apologize, made me uncomfortable in the way of our first meeting.

—I just wanted not to leave college without saying good-bye to you.

—That's all you wanted, she said, smiling not quite at me. You just wanted to say good-bye. You had nothing else in mind but saying good-bye.

I felt that she was mocking me and that I deserved to be mocked. —Is there something wrong with that? I asked.

—For some reason I have trouble accepting the ingenuous pose of that question, she said. Why, I wonder, is that?

Finally, I held my hand out to her and she studied it for a moment before turning herself around and hurrying away.

The next part is a story occasioned from Didi's obit, which travels close to the line of what happened, allowing for the evasions of embarrassment and the tics of the imagination.

2.
B writes a condolence letter—the same letter—to the two surviving daughters, apologizing for intruding on their grief with his own, identifying himself as an old friend of their mother who has been out of touch for the longest time. He isn't sure why he is writing or

why he presumes to have something to tell them about a person they surely knew more intimately than he ever did. Of course he knew her before their time so to speak and so his recollections might provide a different perspective. He is writing because he feels compelled to write and there is no one else to whom he might address such a correspondence. Though he knows nothing of their lives beyond what is reported in the brief obituary in the Times, he feels (presumptuously, he concedes) that they are fortunate to have had such a mother, a woman so vivid that all these years later he could still conjure her in memory, a woman who (so it always seemed to him) had an extraordinary capacity for being in the world. A generous-spirited, openhearted, uncompromising woman of exceptional poise and presence. He elaborates as tactfully as a predilection to hyperbole allows, and he concludes the letter by saying that if there is anything he can do for Didi's daughters in this time of loss, please draw on him as they would an old friend of the family. Under his signature, he adds his address and unlisted phone number.

 He composes the letter as if in a dream, the words coming from some secret source, and he mails both copies before giving the issue a rational second thought. Two days after the jubilant posting, it strikes him how foolish and inappropriate his gesture must seem to the daughters, to anyone in fact living outside his head.

Three weeks later on the same day (oddly), he gets responses from both of Didi's girls. The first letter he opens, which is from the younger daughter, Deidre, is one of those ritual by the numbers notes (spuriously personalized), thanking him for his kind considerations. The other from Deborah Kovaleski-Green is a different proposition altogether.

 —I never liked my mother especially, it starts, never really got on with her. I must be out of my mind telling you this, but there's something in your inappropriate letter that makes me think you'd understand. It goes on to list her grievances against her mother: career taking priority over family, self-involvement, cruelty to her father (whom she separated from when Deborah was fifteen), indifference bordering on negligence to the daughters (herself in particular), radical mood swings, erratic displays of affection. Whenever they got together in recent years, they tended to fight over the most inconsequential things. Even after her mother's illness, the fights continued, though in muted form. They had never had opportunity to make peace with one another—there had been no forgiveness on either side. She was said to be like her mother, which she had only recently accepted as possibly true. She would like to meet with him if that was doable to get his distanced positive view of her mother in greater detail. She would be grateful to him if he could make the time. As a postscript she adds that she had read several of his books and found them very sympathetic. She leaves two phone numbers—home and work—and signs off, Your friend, Debby Kovaleski-Green.

 B rereads the letter several times, rereads it as if it were one of those difficult post-modern texts that needed decoding, though was essentially untranslatable. Of course he is gratified that she wants to see him, though he is uncomfortable carrying his gesture any further than it has gone. That is, he is so eager to see the daughter, he suspects they'd both be better off if it didn't happen.

 B has begun to keep a notebook of recollections concerning Didi, which he rereads and comments on as if it were someone else's story. It has become an issue of faith with him that had he not broken with Didi, had they married, perhaps had children together, his life would have taken a different, happier, course. No other woman, none of his wives, had meant as much to him as Didi had. In losing her, as he sees it, he has lost the essential thing. As a result of her dying, he has had taken from him the last remote possibility of regaining what he had lost.

 B goes through a week long argument with himself before responding to Debby's letter. He makes no mention of her offer to meet with him in person, but talks again about his memories of Didi, elaborating on things he has already written. He thanks her for the "openness and generosity" of her letter and adds—this at the very end—that the voice of the letter seems very much like her mother's voice as he remembers it, which means that without her being conscious of it a reconciliation had taken place between mother and daughter in that Debby had "lovingly assumed certain qualities of her mother into herself."

After he sends the letter, B feels disburdened for a few days as if his letter has somehow set things right in the universe.

Her answer comes by return mail. That is, his letter comes back to him with a handwritten appendage at the bottom.

—Does this mean you don't want to meet with me or what? is the full extent of her message.

He rereads his own letter, feeling rebuffed by its return, trying to decipher what she means by her answer. At the same time, he recognizes that appending a note to his letter and returning it is something Didi might have done in a similar situation. Didi had a gift for deflating the self-important gesture.

B sends back his returned letter, with an appended answer attached to her appended query. —I don't know that I have anything to tell you about your mother that you don't know, but I'm available to meet with you if you still think it will be useful.

A week or so later, B gets a phone call from a woman who sounds like Didi (or as he remembers her) and a few days after that they meet for dinner at a neighborhood bistro on the upper west side.

He is looking for someone who resembles Didi so when a small dumpy woman walks up to him and introduces herself as —Your former girlfriend's daughter, B has a sense of dislocation. This can't be Didi's child. Though he makes a belated effort at concealment, he is unable to hide his initial shock at the daughter's appearance.

—Not what you expected, right? she says. Sorry to disappoint. When I said I was like my mother I didn't mean I looked like her.

B goes through the motions of being gracious, not his strong suit, holds the door for her as they enter the restaurant (though they bump into each other exchanging places). As soon as they are seated, a young woman (much prettier than his companion) comes over to take their orders. B orders a glass of Merlot while Debby opts for a vodka cranberry. —I don't hold my liquor well, she tells him, giggling after the first sip.

—Then maybe you should stop drinking, he says.

—What are you up to these days? she asks B.

B

—I'm working on a long story that threatens to become a novel, he hears himself say. I used to teach at Queens College, but I took early retirement.

—Uh huh, she says as if his comments bore out her preconception of him. I'm a therapist. I've spent so much time in therapy, it seemed the inevitable next step to become a shrink myself. What did you teach?

—I taught writing, he says.

—What else! she says. I gather from your letter that your relationships with women after my mother have not been happy ones.

B starts to object, but she waves him off. —Why else would you be nostalgic about a woman you've had no contact with for almost forty years.

—I loved your mother, he says, surprised at the anger in his voice. Your mother and I loved each other.

—And what about the others? On one of your book jackets, it says you'd been married three times.

—You can't believe everything you read on the back of book jackets, he says.

—You deny that you've been married three times?

—Those are just biographical facts, he says. I happen to think your mother and I might have made a life together.

—Spare me, she says. My guess is, that the two of you wouldn't have lasted more than two or three years if that long.

—What's that judgment based on? he asks.

—My sense of the two of you, she says.

She is about to elaborate on this perception when the waitress comes by to describe the specials of the day. B orders the shitake mushroom appetizer and the monkfish on a bed of spinach. Debby says she is not very hungry and orders the calimari salad, which is an appetizer, as her main course. She also has a second vodka cranberry and eventually a third. Before the coffee and dessert arrive, Debby begins to nod, her eyes flickering shut, her head moving closer and closer to the table. A vague snoring sound, a kind of stereophonic counterpoint, seems to come from some other corner of the room.

B asks her if she's all right and gets a distant sigh in return.

This is not what he hoped their meeting would come to. The waitress comes over after awhile and asks if there is anything she can do to help.

—She's probably just tired, B says.

—I think she's drunk, the waitress says. She had at least three drinks at the bar before you got here and from what I could tell she'd been drinking before that. Do you know where she lives? I'll call a car service for you if you like.

B looks in his jacket pocket for the letter Debby sent him and is relieved to find it, but the return address is blurred by a water stain.

The waitress shakes Debby's shoulder. —Where do you live, honey? she asks.

—You don't need to do that, Debby mumbles. She opens her eyes and lifts her head with the flourish of a circus performer doing something obscurely difficult. I live a few blocks away. I'm a neighborhood person.

B settles the tab and leaves the restaurant with Debby holding on to his arm.

—I can make it on my own, she tells him, but he insists on accompanying her home.

—How do I know you're not some dirty old man who is only pretending to have known my mother? she asks as they stand in front of her door, Debby searching through her purse for the key.

When she gets the door open, B is eager to return to his uneventful privacy, but Debby invites him in, holding on to his sleeve to emphasize her point. B does not try hard enough to get away and finds himself inside Debby's dramatically over-decorated apartment—the motif is theatrical masks—the door closed behind them.

—I should get home, he says, wondering why he doesn't just go. There seems no longer any necessity for him to stay with her.

They are sitting next to each other on her living room couch and Debby rests her head on his shoulder. B is trying to figure out what is going on between them. He imagines Didi looking on from wherever.

—Do you want to go to bed with me? she asks.

—No, he says.

—Beware, she says. This offer may not be tended in your presence ever again. I'll present the question one more time. Do you or do you not want to go to bed with me?

—I make it a rule, B says, not to go to bed with women who are not responsible for their behavior.

She puzzles over his answer. —Is that yes or no? she asks.

—It's no, he says.

—Then I'll thank you to leave, she says, disappearing from the room.

3.

B is glad to get out of there, though once he hits the street he considers going back. Didi would appreciate his looking after her daughter, he tells himself. At the same time, he can't imagine (or can imagine too well) what direction such looking after might take. So, disappointed in human nature, his own and others, he goes home, concerned with getting a good night's sleep, which of course he won't get anyway, never does.

For the next few days, Debby and B chat on the phone as if they have known each other for years. Her manner assumes an intimacy which he finds disconcerting, though he is secretly flattered. —I'll take you to dinner at a nice place, he tells her, but you have to remain sober.

—Are you afraid I'll embarrass you? she asks.

—When you get drunk you embarrass yourself, he says.

—If I knew you were a fucking bleeding heart, she says, I never would have answered your letter in the first place. The fact is, drinking protects me from feeling embarrassed. He can see that there is something to that, but of course once she sobers up (which may be why she stays drunk) the embarrassment she's been avoiding will hit her twice as hard.

—Come with me to a AA meeting, he says.

—If I was going to go to an AA meeting, she says, why would I need you there to hold my hand?

—I need you there to hold my hand, he says.

—For a supposedly sophisticated person, you're a real cornball, she says.

So a relationship evolves between them, a casual insult-freighted friendship. B finds himself spending more time on the telephone with Didi's daughter than with either of his own sons.

One day, his older son comes by to visit, which is a rare occasion. —I worry about you, Dad, his son says. You live like a hermit. Nothing's going on in your life.

—Nothing that you know about, B says. I'm seeing someone.

—Whoever she is, the son says, from the look of your apartment, I would bet she doesn't do housework.

—She's never been here, B says, annoyed at the remark on several accounts. And if I thought my apartment needed cleaning, I'd hire someone.

—Dad, says the son, who is this person you're seeing that has never been to your place and doesn't do windows?

—When I'm ready to tell you, you'll be the first to know, B says.

The son says this is not meant to be a duel of wits, not on his part, that his visit has been an expression of concern on his part, that he and Danton have been worried about B's unavailability since his retirement.

—Hey, I've been cultivating my garden, B says. And I've been seeing someone.

—Okay, who have you been seeing? he says. It's just that I have difficulty believing what you say is true. From what I can tell, Dad, is that you've been alone too much and that you've been depressed.

—How can someone as out of control as you be a therapist? B says to Debby over dinner at Café des Artistes.

—The reason I'm so good at it, Debby tells him, is that my openness to my own problems enhances insight into the problems of others.

B, who has dipped his toe into therapy on a few harried occasions, remains skeptical of her claim. —I worry about you, he says. I think you need someone to take you in hand.

—We call that projecting, she says. You're a lonely man, B. And why shouldn't you be? It's not the most fun in the world living alone.

—Now who's projecting, B says. He is holding her hand when he makes this remark. His sense of her attractiveness, or lack of it, has been revised in the three months that have passed since their first meeting. She is smaller and less svelte than her mother, but certainly sexy to the eye (and whatever) of this beholder. The fact of it is, he has not even so much as kissed her (mouth to mouth) at this point. His relationship to her has been a kind of loco parentis undermined by an occasional flirtation. Debby continues to insist that if he had married her mother, they wouldn't have lasted three years together. Why three years, he wonders, but doesn't ask. What is it about him that suggests that three years is the longest he could survive with anyone (he has been married over 7 years three times to other difficult women)?

—If you have such a jaundiced opinion of me, he says, why do you continue to see me?

She waves off the question as if it were unworthy of consideration.

—In your professional opinion, how long would you and I survive together? he asks.

She takes back her hand, squinches her eyes at him.

—Are you just babbling or is that question supposed to mean something?

B is not so much surprised at her belligerence as he is surprised at the injudiciousness of his remarks. Indeed, he is innocent (or at least oblivious) of his own intentions.

—I was thinking about what you said about your mother and I not lasting three years together. I apologize if my question offended you.

—I don't think you and I would last one hour, she says, because it's unlikely in the extreme that we'd ever live together. I mean, what gives you the idea that I would even consider moving in with you?

B holds up his hands in a gesture of surrender. —I didn't think you would consider moving in with me. It was a hypothetical question I was asking. We do spend a lot of time talking on the phone.

—Maybe that's because we're both lonely, she says. And we want something from each other that we're obviously not getting.

B is wary of asking, knows and doesn't know, what mutual lack she is referring to. They are not making it together is what she means. The idea of sleeping with his former girl friend's daughter is disturbing to him, though it is not anything he wants to confide in her. So he changes the subject which elicits a knowing smile from Debby as if she had seen his brand of evasive tactics in her professional practice too many times before.

4.
It is a fact that I have always felt lonely even when living with someone, even when married. I tended to marry women who wouldn't encroach on my lonely space. The remote Clara. And later Genevieve who tended to value only those things she didn't have. This is something Debby knew about me from the first without being thrown any telltale clues. The mystery was that, while feeling lonely—it was like a deeply muted pain—I nevertheless dodged intimacy like a fatal bullet homed at my heart. I was so used to living alone, I didn't know how much I truly minded it. The unacknowledged truth is, I find comfort in being alone and at the same time I can barely stand it. A certain pride is achieved by enduring the all but unendurable thing. Have I never not been lonely? The early days with Genevieve perhaps, though I'm not sure even of that.

5.
B asks Debby to spend New Years eve with him, but she has a prior commitment, or so she says. An hour later she calls back. —Just

what exactly did you have in mind for us? she asks.

—Does that mean you've become available, B says, or is it just a matter of finding out what you might be missing?

—If we spend New Years eve together, you're going to have to go to bed with me, she says.

B has an answer to everything. —Wouldn't our making such an agreement take all the spontaneity out of it?

—Take a hike, she says.

—If you're going to be uncompromising, B says, I suppose I'll have to accept your terms. But you have to promise me you'll remain sober for the entire evening.

B goes to her place for a home-cooked meal and then to a party of mostly people his age or older. Debby wanders about nursing a Perrier with a squiggle of lime, speaking only when spoken to, and even then stopping only to answer the question put to her. It is not B's intention to drink too much, but since he does, (he is already on his third glass of champagne), he knows dimly that he will be held accountable afterward. Perhaps he is drinking too much because Debby is not drinking at all, a way of representing the firm while one of its members is on vacation.

A friend, a former lover, tells him why she is breaking up with the man she has lived with for the past five years. B is keeping track of her argument while watching Debby's perambulations out of the corner of his eye. She is leaving him, she says, for political reasons. He is in favor of the death penalty. She does not see herself spending the rest of her life with a man who gets off on institutional murder. Her reasons seem false or unduly severe, but it is not B's part to tell her that.

Debby comes out of nowhere, tugs on his arm, whispers, —Time to go, Bo.

The woman he has been talking to, stops in mid sentence, says, —I'll thank you not to repeat this to anyone.

Debby says, holding out her hand to the other woman, —We haven't been introduced.

B takes the occasion to turn away and slip like a secret into the wall-to-wall crowd. Moments later, frozen on the edge of a conversation among strangers, he feels Debby's hand on his arm just above the elbow. –You can't escape me, she says. I hope you're not really trying.

6.

At some point B feels obliged to introduce Debby to his two sons. The fateful moment comes three days after he has spent the night in her apartment and the day after they have agreed to look for a larger apartment they might live in together. Telling his sons, he hopes, will validate a relationship that has never seemed quite real to him. Aware of the apparent inappropriateness of this alliance, B seeks to set up an ideal situation for the meeting. Debby suggests having them to dinner at her place, and a date is set and invitations made.

The dinner is a disaster. Debby gets drunk and falls into her verbally abusive mode, accusing the sons of not giving B the affection due him. The sons struggle to be polite, but at some point the younger son, Danton, walks out without a word, his dinner barely acknowledged. His absence creates an odd tension around the table. The older son gets up after a while (before coffee and dessert are served) and says that he too has to leave.

–Why do you hate your father? Debby asks him.

–This has nothing to do with my father, he says.

–I don't need to be talked to that way in my own house, she says to him. You have my permission to get the fuck out of here.

B intercedes, takes the son into the hall to talk to him. –She's not like this when she's sober, he tells him. Be patient with her, okay? She has a drinking problem.

–She asked me to leave, Dad, the son says. If I go back, she's only going to throw me out again.

B acknowledges the son's point, decides not to press the issue any further.

–You don't have to stay either, she says when B returns. No one's forcing you to stay here against your will. She walks into the kitchen and he follows after her, claiming her by the sink, wrapping his arms around her as if his hug were the only thing keeping her from going into orbit.

—You're a mess, he says in her ear.

—Look who's talking, she says. You're the world's doormat, fellow. There's been so much shit wiped off on you you've been passing it off as suntan.

When he lets go of her, she collapses to the floor in what seems to B a kind of slow motion. He lifts her up, eliciting a moan and some under the breath curses. When it is clear that she is out for the count, he carries her into the bedroom, removes her shoes and rolls her under the comforter. He wants to leave but he clears off the dining table first, scraping the dishes and piling them on the counter next to the sink. He puts plastic wrap over the leftover food and makes awkward room for it in the oversubscribed refrigerator.

On the drive home, he thinks about their first sexual tangle together, which was two weeks ago, and concedes that it was a lot less harrowing for him in actuality (is harrowing the right word?) than it had been in the imagination. In fact, the sex had been rather playful and lighthearted. Up until the actual moment they did the deed, B imagined he had been seeing Debby in part at least as a favor to Didi, the repayment of some kind of unacknowledged debt. After sleeping with Didi's daughter, that illusion of course would no longer fly.

He imagines Didi observing his behavior and registering disappointment. She must feel justified, he thinks—why shouldn't she?—in having lived her adult life apart from him. He was untrustworthy, as she had guessed, a slave to the itch of impulse and indifference. Lying in his bed at night, nurturing his aloneness, he asks Didi to forgive him as if she were invisibly in the room and could puzzle out his thoughts.

—You have it all wrong, she says, sidling under the covers next to him. There's never been anyone in my life but you.

—Is that right? he says. His exhilaration almost stopping his breath. He doesn't dare reach out for her.

—Of course it's not right, she says. I had a husband, I had other lovers, I had children. You were the farthest thing from my thoughts all those years. I said what I did just to see what you would make of it. You just think everything's about you or we wouldn't even be having this conversation.

—Wait a minute, B says, why are you haunting me if I am the farthest thing from your thoughts? Huh?

She pretends to ignore him, which confirms him in his nostalgia.

He is aware that the conversation between them is delusion, but that doesn't mean he is ready to give it up. She is facing away and he locks his arms around her from behind.

—I am not haunting you by choice, she says. This is all your selfish doing, you impossible man. After despoiling my daughter, I wouldn't think you'd have the gall to talk to me again.

The more she abuses him (more or less, what difference does it make?), the happier it makes him. And B has never been a happy man except for a few barely acknowledged isolated moments. Are you through with me? she asks. Can I go now?

—Never, he says.

And they go on that way, arguing over the dead past, announcing feelings or denying them, B with a commemorative hard-on, elated by nostalgia, until he wakes from this dream, or falls asleep in mid-sentence, losing her again once and for all, one or the other, whichever is truer to the story.

XII. OUTTAKES

My mother would say with a kind of embarrassed pride when she presented me to one of her friends that I was large for my age. It was not exactly true. In school, as I remember, when they lined us up in size place for the class picture, I was the fifth shortest boy in the class.

B offers this story about his mother in group after this smug guy, Phil, asks him why the only parent he ever talks about is his father.

—The reason you don't think about your mom, Phil says, is that you're so angry at her, it's safer to shut her out.

B says, —Bullshit.

—Come on, Phil says. I can't believe this is news to you. Your mother was the first woman to break your heart.

—You're in denial, the woman he has a crush on in the group says.

Nothing gets B angrier than to be told he's in denial. Nothing. —What am I denying? he asks the room. I happen to think there's something sweet about a mother seeing her son as larger than other boys his age even if it was a false perception. She eventually lost her memory, my mother did, and this may have been the earliest stages. At some point, probably more gradually than we realized, she stopped being there, the inner person disappeared as if its only existence was the sum of its lost memories. Even when she was out of it and didn't know who you were, she was gracious enough to pretend that she did. Everyone who knew my mother, without exception, liked her. The group is silent when he finishes this tirade and he looks around him fiercely, hoping to frighten off attack before it catches him unaware.

—

B woke abruptly from a dream of flight to find himself in bed—hers (theirs)—next to Heather, his friend Max's wife. They were lying back to back, his right foot entwined with her left, though they were otherwise unconnected. The shock of being where he dared not go nearly stopped his heart. He couldn't for the life of him recall the steps leading to his present disgrace. The first thing he did was peer at his watch—that is, the first thing after he carefully disentangled his foot—and it seemed to show ten after four, or possibly twenty after two. Having the time, even if imperfectly—it was too dark really to tell—gave him a purchase on reality. His idea was to get out of Max and Heather's bed before Heather discovered him there, but on the other hand he didn't feel much like moving. An enervating lethargy had settled in. It wasn't so much that he was too comfortable to move as that he couldn't imagine a preferable alternative. Going out in the cold to chase down his car—he had difficulty remembering these days where he parked—didn't seem like much fun. The rash of red flowers that dotted the comforter that covered him to the waist seemed to glow in the dark.

Look, you really have to get out of here, he told himself, and you have to do it without waking Heather. When he lifted the corner of the comforter to slide his left leg free and following that, his right, Heather mumbled something that might have been, –Work ethic, and moved spasmodically toward his side of the bed, resettling herself. He held his breath until he was almost sure that she was asleep before completing his journey from bed to floor. A misjudged move ended with him rolling on to the carpet with a painful thump, his left elbow taking the brunt of the fall.

He lay where he had fallen, listening to Heather shuffle about on the bed, wondering if he had damaged himself in any notable

B

way. He couldn't be sure but he had the sneaking suspicion that he was lying on his shoes.

—

This woman of a certain age, one of the faculty wives perhaps, gets B into a corner and insists on telling him about her marriage. —We fucked once, she says, in the 27 years we've been married and I have twins to show for it. I'd say that was efficiency, wouldn't you?

—I see, B says, looking around the room for Y whose hand he thinks he notices emerging through the crowd to grab an *hors d'oeuvre* from the center table.

—You don't know anything about it, the woman says. How can you possibly? I'm the only one in the world that knows what it's like to have been in this marriage.

—I hear what you're saying, B says. Still, it's hard to believe that in all the time you and your husband, the dean (the name eludes him) have been together, you've only slept with him once.

—Now you're being overly literal, she says. There may have been as many as three sexual encounters between us in the years we've lived together and I've conveniently forgotten two of them

—Uh huh, B says, only half listening. I probably should get myself another drink.

—Take mine, she says, exchanging glasses with him. Do you mind if I ask you a personal question? B clears his throat.

—How often do you and your wife have sex? she asks, leaning into him as if she means to pass her words from mouth to mouth. B hesitates, flees the room with Y in tow on the playing fields of the imagination.

—If you'd rather not say, I understand, she says. Still and all, I'd be willing to bet it's more than three times in thirty years.

—My wife and I have separated, B says. Recently.

—Good for her, the woman says. Or maybe you're the one who did the leaving. Which is it? You're probably too much of a gentleman to say. I don't meant to be forward which you'd know was not my style if you knew me better, but if you're looking to get out of here which I suspect you are we could continue our *tête à tête* at my house, which is a stroll from the college.

—I don't know, B says.

—It doesn't matter to me one way or another what you decide, she says. So please, I'm asking this as a favor, don't take my feelings into consideration. Please make your decision on coming to my place solely on what it flatters you to do.

—Thank you for the invitation, B says, but I'm here with someone. An abrupt desperate glance at the dwindling group of celebrants in the room gives the lie to that assertion.

—

Although the snow was falling in almost invisible flurries, the stuff was sticking to the ground, was accumulating more quickly than he would have supposed. Last time B checked his watch his son was 10 minutes late. He held up his wrist to the streetlight, but it was hard to make out the time through the glaze of snow. He thought of going indoors, but his son would be showing up at any moment and so it seemed best to keep vigil at the appointed spot.

Dusted with snow, the people arriving at the Garden mostly in groups of two seemed ghostlike and B had the sense of recognizing one or another from some forgotten past with only the vaguest sense of their occasion in his life. Of course New York was full of people you had met—at parties, at theaters, at movies, at concerts, at sporting events, at supermarkets even—without having exchanged a word or shaken a hand.

A woman went by (with three younger women) who looked like someone he had once met at a meeting of a group called Heartbreak Anonymous. He whispered her name, Helena, to her back as she passed and though she went on without turning his way, he sensed from her body language that some connection had been made.

A burly man he was sure he didn't know stopped in front of B and said to him, —Aren't you...? I just want to say the city needs more people like you. The man, who was redfaced and may have been slightly drunk, shook his hand vigorously then hurried away.

A woman he did know, a former student from years back, said hello as she ambled by with her boyfriend or husband, then returned to say she had enjoyed the two classes she took with him but there were times she had absolutely no idea what he was talking about. It made her feel stupid, she said, which was not good for her self-esteem.

Then he was sure he heard his son's voice, saying, —Dad, sorry, and he excused himself to the former student, still wondering what he might have said that was beyond her comprehension, and turned in the direction of his son's voice, the swirling snow blinding B momentarily.

—I thought we'd have dinner first, B said to the approaching ghost. But the snow-dusted figure hardly looked at him as he flurried by, muttering something to himself that sounded like —Fuck-all, though of course it could have been anything.

—

B walks two blocks in the heavy rain-bordering-on-hail with the redheaded Cassandra Lutz at his side. —I have something to ask you, she says, whispering into his bad ear. What's your sign?

—My sign? You mean my astrological sign, don't you? I used to know it. If you tell me what signs there are, I'm sure it'll come back to me.

—Tell me your birth date and I'll tell you what your sign is, she says. That's an easier way of doing it.

His birth date is part of the public record but for some incomprehensible reason he feels the need to guard this information.

—It's not something I put much credence in, he says. Astrological readings. Can't we just let the matter drop?

—Everyone says that until I've done a reading for them, she says. This is not going to hurt, I promise you, okay? You'll be surprised at how much you learn about yourself. I have a reputation for doing the most empowering readings in the business.

—I don't doubt your skill, he says. I'm just not interested.

—Your close-minded stubbornness tells me that you're either a Scorpio or an Aries, she says. You could also be a Leo, though I wouldn't bet on it.

At this point they get into an excessively polite argument,

which evolves into a shouting match as if they were some long term dysfunctional married couple, standing on a street corner in the rain with nowhere to go that would make a difference. Cassandra's parting remark as she storms off is, —And I was just beginning to feel attracted to you.

—

—Don't you know how attracted I am to you, Penny says. She is lying on top of B fully clothed in the back seat of his rented Dodge Polara parked on a semi-dark corner of a dead end street. He imagines the look of astonishment on the face of someone—a cop perhaps shining a flashlight in the window—observing them. Of course sometimes imagination dovetails with reality. Someone does tap at the window just as Penny has reached inside his fly to take his member (of an inexclusive club) in her humid hand. In short order his fly is rezipped and B is sitting up, his edgy attention directed at the window at which the tapping sound appeared. The tap does not repeat and B, disentangling himself, feels the need to feign innocence, a precaution directed from childhood memories of humiliation. An uneventful minute passes before B thinks to unroll the window.

—It's just kids, Penny says, but B remains wary despite the fact that whoever interrupted them is gone.

—Why don't we go to my hotel room? he says.

—I don't know, she says. It just seems like so much trouble. It's fine here, it really is. She unzips his fly and goes down on him, his shoulder cramped against an arm rest. B warily accedes to pleasure, his shoulder aching in counterpoint, while dangerous shadows surround their fragile sanctuary.

—

His father, carrying a pint of something in a brown paper bag, hurrying by B's parked car, stops in his tracks to glance at B slumped down behind the wheel. —If your car won't start, you can borrow mine, he says. What are you doing sitting there by yourself like that? I thought you had to be at school.

B

B turns the key and his old Saab bursts into voice. As he pulls out of the space, he electronically slides down the driver-side window and he waves to his father. –I'll call you, Dad, he says. As he reaches the stop sign at the corner and looks back through the rear view mirror, he sees his father, frozen in place, shaking his head in disapproval as if it were a replay of some unremembered scene from childhood. On the drive back, an idea for a story blows into his head in which a grown man, returning from an extended trip, arrives home to find himself as a child, sitting cross-legged on the floor waiting anxiously for his father's return.

—

B hadn't expected to see her again, had barely thought of Gladys Fleur since his disastrous performance at the Femmes Club but there she was (smaller than life) waiting on line to buy a ticket at the Angelica Film Complex.

He called her name. –Gladys, Gladys Fleur, and she looked at him without a stir of recognition, offering an embarrassed smile in compensation.

–Yes? she said, squinting.

–Are you alone? he asked her.

–I don't know if that's any of your business, she said in that severe voice he remembered from their first conversation on the phone.

–I can see you don't remember me, he said, moving alongside her as if he were her partner in line. I spoke at a Femmes Club meeting about three months ago and made such a mess of things you had to lead me out the back way for my protection. If you knew me better, you would know I was not as incorrigible as I seemed that night. At this point they were almost at the cashier's box and Gladys's usually impassive face seemed virtually carved in stone.

–Incorrigible is a fancy word, she said. I would have used the more down to earth "asshole" in its place. Turning away from him, she requested a ticket for the very movie he had also come to see, which reignited his fantasy about their secret affinity.

She was already out of the picture by the time he purchased his ticket, but moments later he found himself, although he had willfully kept his distance, three steps behind her on the escalator going up to the third level. His feelings wounded by her rebuff, he decided to honor her wish to be alone (or at least unencumbered by his presence). Not wanting to give the impression of dogging her steps, he went into the Men's room and washed his hands, making every effort to avoid looking at the tormented face in the mirror, which persisted in catching his eye.

  He dawdled at the door to the theater, bent over twice to adjust the tie on his left shoe. Several filmgoers and three minutes passed before he made his delayed entrance. The house lights were dimming as he opened the door and a coming attraction for a whimsical British comedy was unfolding on the screen. It took a moment for his eyes to adjust to the semi-darkness—the theater about half full—before moving confidently down the aisle. Someone bumped him from behind. —Hey, he complained.

  —You're so slow, a voice whispered, and perhaps it was his fault, the incidental contact, for stopping abruptly. A second somewhat more aggressive bump followed the first. Feeling mildly aggrieved, he willed himself not to turn, not to confront his ostensible assailant, focusing instead on choosing a seat on the aisle a few rows from the screen. As soon as he had crossed his legs, he had to uncross them and get up to let the person behind enter his row. During this transaction, he resisted glancing at the woman sliding by him, though he couldn't help but be aware she had slipped into the seat immediately next to his.

  A voice whispered to him during the closure of the second coming attraction. —I have no idea what came over me that time, she seemed to say, emphasizing the word *time*. They had kissed in the corridors of the Fort Hamilton Armory and then she had slapped his face. He wondered, reaching for her hand, to which of those gestures her apology (if that's what it was) referred.

—

It was a few minutes past One a.m. in the new year when they got to Debby's apartment, B wondering how he might break his promise to sleep with her without seeming to go back on his word. When

B

Debby said, —You don't have to, you know, if you don't want to, his feelings in the matter did a 360-degree turn. It was not that he didn't want to fuck her, but some moral compunction gave him pause. She was after all the daughter of the first woman he had ever loved.

Debby took off her clothes while B watched shyly, his eyes partially averted. —What you see is what you get, she said or, as the case may be, don't get. B went into the bathroom to brush his teeth. He noted that Debby had an electric tooth brush and he elected to use his finger instead.

When he emerged—he had also undressed down to his briefs in the bathroom—Debbie was submerged under the covers, a thin white blanket over her head.

—What's going on? he asked her, moving around to the unoccupied side of the bed, shivering slightly in the overheated room. The blanket muffled whatever it was she had to say.

—Got you sucker, it might have been as he made his way under the covers. A nervous laugh ruffled the white blanket. He lifted the cover as though it was an upside down veil and kissed her, missing her mouth by no more than an inch.

—

His inquisitor was an intense woman with touched-up blond hair somewhere in the neighborhood of forty-five.

Q: Do you mind if I leave the tape machine on during our discussion. I don't do shorthand and my memory, so they tell me, is not the greatest.

B: Actually, I do mind. I'm sorry to be so difficult, but I get self-conscious when I know I'm being recorded.

Q: Why don't we talk awhile with the machine off and when you get comfortable, when I can see that you're comfortable I'll turn it on. Okay?

B: I'd prefer that you didn't.

Q: I just don't want to run the risk of misquoting you. Okay? Let me say before we start, though I admire your work, as a woman and a feminist, there are certain things in your books that I find objectionable.

B is about to say something that might confirm her worst opinion of him, though instead he offers an apologetic shrug. The tape registers 20 seconds of silence.

Q: Let me play devil's advocate for a moment if I may. If your books don't seem real to the reader, why should he bother reading them?

B: I think the devil would be pleased at how well you're representing him.

Q: No, seriously. Isn't it the illusion that we are participating in a real world, one that is less humdrum than the one we live in that attracts most readers to the novel?

B: I can't speak for most readers. I write novels that someone like myself might want to read. Novels that frankly confess themselves to be pieces of fabrication and that don't try to deceive an unwary reader into believing otherwise.

Q: I don't see you as a writer who writes consciously out of personal experience, though marriage and divorce seem a recurrent issue in your work and also, from the biographical data available, in your life.

B: I avoid writing out of my life as much as I can, but what else is there. I mean it draws on you if you refuse to draw on it. Generally, I'm more comfortable with what appears to be invented material. If I know in advance what's going to happen, I tend to lose interest. Whatever my intentions for a work, the unconscious is always skulking around, insisting on its prerogatives.

Q: In your most recent book, *An Unauthorized Life*, you create a character whose biographical information resembles your own though is different in certain verifiable respects. It seems to me the point you're making is that all biography is fictitious to some extent and that fiction, if it's doing its job, needs to be true in its own way. Does what I'm saying mean anything to you?

B: The character in *An Unauthorized Life* was intended as a shadow self, a worse and better alternative with whom I happen to share certain experiences in broad outline. Of course, the same thing might be said about my relationship to the central figures in my other books.

Q: Madame Bovary, *c'est moi*?

B: If you will.

Q: Are you one of those writers who objects to readers who don't respond to him on the highest levels?

B: When you put it that way, I can only say I hope not. I see myself at least in part as an entertainer and sometimes even as a frustrated stand-up comic. Of course my limited readership indicates that this is not a widely shared opinion.

Q: Well, a number of my expectations for this interview have been deflated. I had heard that you would be difficult and so far, except for the business about the mike, you've been a pussycat. I was also told, I won't mention by who, that you would make a pass at me before the interview was done. That seemed possible because your alter-ego in *An Unauthorized Life* would probably have done as much in a comparable situation. In fact, in real life so to speak, you've been a perfect gentleman.

B: That's the problem, isn't it? Writers find it hard to be themselves in real life.

—

Word reached B that his former wife was working on a novel that touched on the break up of their marriage. The following is the opening of an early draft of the manuscript as he imagined it.

It's true that I had fallen in love with Sam, who was also my husband's friend and that I tried to keep B from knowing (and did my damndest to make it so obvious that only someone emotionally blind would miss the point), that I told B I could no longer live with him, that's true too, that in my heart's text I had erased all traces of him from my life, all that is undeniable, but B was not blameless in all this. For one, he was altogether too eager to take what I said in the most literal light. For two, for reasons of denial, he couldn't assimilate that my disaffection was irreversible and not susceptible to changes in the weather. I had a list of grievances as long as your arm. I hated B for every reason I could conceive, some in obvious contradiction to others. Hate of course is a great uniter of oppositions. I mourned his absence, I grieved for his death, and I wondered—this, the most troubling of all—how someone who wasn't there could take up so much space. These conflicted feelings, for which he was responsible, embittered me.

 One night, he came home from his therapy group and discovered me on the phone talking to my lover. When he came toward me, I motioned him to go away. He left the room but then almost immediately returned. For someone who didn't exist, he was everywhere. I again motioned him to leave me in peace. He took a threatening posture, which made me laugh. –He won't let us talk, I said into the phone. I'll call you back after he goes to sleep.

 After I hung up the phone, he knocked over a chair and moved off, hunched over with the weight of his defeat. –Big man, I heard myself say in no voice I had ever used before. You're nothing. You're nothing. You're nothing.

 How much I felt for him at that moment!

XIII. WEDDINGS

1.
B is dancing with a former wife, the mother of the bride, at his daughter's wedding. This is her second wedding, his daughter's second wedding, and the former wife he is dancing with is the second of his three former wives. He wonders if there isn't some imponderable significance in the numerical coincidence.

Though he can't really dance, they are playing something slow and he enjoys the risks involved, the embarrassment avoided, in faking his way through.

–One thing we always did well together, his ex says, is dance.

–You know, he says, I can't remember ever dancing with you before.

–How is that supposed to make me feel, she says. I remember three occasions at least that we danced together. My sister's wedding for one. You danced with everyone that night.

–I accept your version, he says, wanting for the sake of the occasion to avoid a fight, though his dancing with everyone, as she puts it, seems out of character.

–You were in your cups that evening, she says. That's why you don't remember anything. If you hadn't had a few drinks, you probably wouldn't be dancing with me now. She likes to dispute and what he does remember of their marriage was the endless succession of petty squabbles they had in the seven almost eight years they endured together.

–I can tell from the way you're dancing, she stage whispers, that you're doing this out of obligation. I don't need that from you. I really don't. There is a live orchestra—a combo really—and the songs go on longer than the anticipated three minutes, sometimes sliding from one into another like a medley, making it difficult to determine the conclusion of one dance and the beginning of the next.

—Are you getting tired? he asks her.

—Are you looking for a way out? she counters.

Eyes roving idly over his former wife's shoulder, he notices that his daughter, the bride, is dancing with her husband's father and that the man is holding her closer than seems appropriate. He passes on this disturbing observation to his partner. An attractive woman dancing with a much older man winks at B as she glides by.

—You would think that, she says. That's so like you.

—Look for yourself, he says, turning them both around, the move only felicitous in its imagining. They stumble awkwardly into their present configuration, brush into another couple that apologizes as they hit them.

—Do you see what I mean? he asks.

—Everything's a fog without my glasses, she says. Besides, the man's a professional ballroom dancer. It's impersonal. Whatever he's doing is like a doctor's examination.

—Do you really want your daughter to have a medical checkup from a ballroom dancer, he says.

—I'm not going to deal with that, she says.

The fox trot they have been approximating to some unrecognizable old favorite turns into The Anniversary Waltz, the emcee crooning the words in a self-congratulatory way, changing a word here and there to personalize the song. B has taken an instinctive dislike to this other father, this so-called dance pro, and he wonders what the groom makes of his father clutching his bride in this presumptuous way. Out of the corner of his eye, B notices the vapid boy on the sidelines flirting with one of the bridesmaids, Lisa, the sexiest of his daughter's friends. Inappropriate behavior seems to run in the family.

—Isn't it traditional, B says, for the father of the bride to have the first dance with his daughter. His partner issues an exasperated sigh.

B

—That's just the point, she says. They didn't want a traditional wedding. Haven't you heard anything your daughter has said to you.

—When this song is over, I'm going to dance with Sonya, He announces. I hope that doesn't offend the gods of anti-tradition that hold sway here.

—I think that's a perfectly wonderful idea, she says.

—Do you?

—I do. But you need to be careful, you know that don't you, not to ruin this evening for her. A marriage is a fragile thing as who knows better than you. Don't behave the way my father did on our wedding night.

Her remark, the intriguing senselessness of it, reminds B unhappily of old times. —I don't remember your father misbehaving at our wedding, he says, taking the bait.

—That doesn't surprise me, she says. I wonder why. What happened at our wedding, it so happens, determined the ultimate fate of our marriage.

—I don't believe that, he says. What could your father have possibly done that would have such an impact on our marriage?

When she makes a point of not answering him, he rephrases the question.

—Let's forget it, she says. This is the not the time or place to take the skeletons out of the closet. Anyway, it was not so much what my father did that ruined things as what you did in response to what he did.

—I have no idea what you're talking about, he says.

—Of course you don't, she says. That's the whole point. If you did, you might have been able to sustain a relationship with someone.

B's memory of their wedding celebration is shadowy so he is vulnerable to whatever charge of bad conduct she wishes to attribute to him. Still, he'd rather know what she has in mind (crazy as it may be) than to be left hanging. —So? he asks.

—You know more than you're willing to own up to, she says. Whatever else you are, you're not stupid. (Whatever else is he?)

—My memory is a disaster area, he reminds her. I have no

idea what your father did that night that caused such a problem. If it was so troubling, why didn't you say something at the time?

—If you didn't know what it was, there was hardly any point in mentioning it afterward, she says. You do remember that he cut in on us when we were dancing. You do remember that much, don't you?

His will to remember her father cutting in on them while they danced offers him the illusion that he did. He even remembers, or imagines he does, her father tapping him on the shoulder in time-honored fashion. —It did seem a bit competitive of him, B says.

—Then why didn't you stick to your guns? she says bitterly, digging a knuckle into his back.

—How was I to know you didn't want to dance with him?

—That's not the issue, she says, and you know it.

But he doesn't know what the issue is and that, in his view, has always been the problem between them. If you're not in touch with the nuances of her private world, you will inevitably miss the point in some obscurely unredeemable way. He feels a poke in the shoulder blades which irritates him no end, particularly when it repeats a second and third time.

Eventually, he stops dancing and turns to see who wants to cut in. It is the groom's father, the man who had been dancing with his daughter and B yields to him with a mix of relief and reluctance. As soon as the man dances off with his former wife, she gives B an unforgiving glance over her partner's shoulder. He surveys the room, looking for his daughter Sonya who seems to have disappeared at her own wedding. That he can't pick her out of the crowd worries him. He notices that the groom is still chatting with one of his daughter's friends and he ambles over in their direction.

—Have you seen Sonya, Gregg, B asks him.

—I thought she was dancing with you, he says.

—The truth is, we had a fight a half hour ago and we've been avoiding each other since.

—On your wedding day, for God's sake. I've never heard anything so stupid.

—That's the kind of thing my father would say to me, he

says, and walks away as if B had slapped him.

—Sonya's in the Ladies' Room, Mr. B, Lisa says. If you want, I'll go get her for you.

—I can wait until she comes out, he says.

—Suit yourself, Mr. B. I'll tell you this much, I don't think she's coming out any time soon.

—I was hoping to dance with her, he says. You know, the traditional father-daughter dance at a wedding.

—I didn't have a traditional father myself so I don't know anything about that, Lisa says. If you're looking to dance, Mr. B, I'll dance with you.

—That's very kind of you, Lisa...but...

Before the thought is finished they are on the floor doing one of those high energy rock-and-roll dances B usually does his best (or worst) to avoid. He watches what the guy alongside him is doing and imitates his moves. —Way to go, Mr. B, Lisa says.

—What were you and Gregg talking about? B asks her, but the noise of the music and the distance between them makes it hard for her to hear him and she shrugs her response. B shrugs back as if it were a phrase in the dance and after a while he notices the man next to him is also making shrugging gestures.

Lisa flashes him an encouraging smile. B thinks he sees his daughter in the far corner of the room, her back to him, talking to someone from her mother's family. He wants to go to her but it seems unacceptable to break ranks while the music is still holding sway.

When he broke up with his second wife and moved out of the house, Sonya held it against him for the longest time. So he improvises a slide step as if it proceeded inevitably from the shrug, as a means of edging closer to his daughter. Lisa picks up on the slide step after awhile and embellishes on it and so between them they have this complicated series of steps going that takes all his concentration to perform.

Someone bumps him from behind and, in delayed reaction, he loses his balance, finds himself tumbling in slow motion to the glossy wood floor. His right elbow takes the brunt of the hit. When B gets to his feet, the music has stopped and almost everyone on the dance floor seems to be looking his way. Discombobulated, he limps to the sidelines, looking for a place to sit down. As he passes through the crowd, he hears his name echoing in muffled whispers, the tone mildly disdainful, though it's possible, he acknowledges, that they're talking about something else altogether. An elderly woman offers him her seat and he reluctantly declines the offer.

As soon as the pain in his elbow subsides, B resumes his search for Sonya. Though he continues to limp, he has no recollection of hurting his leg. His former wife appears, moving toward him with an urgency that makes him want to run for his life.

—I want you to talk to your daughter, she says.

—I'd be glad to if I could find her, he says.

—This is serious, she says, taking his arm. You have to tell her that she can't leave her marriage because of a silly argument. She won't listen to me. Sonya is standing behind her mother, staring into space, wearing an unconvincing public smile.

—What's the matter, darling? he says.

—Nothing, she says in a small voice.

—We haven't done the traditional father-daughter dance yet, he says. The evening's not complete without it.

—Please, she says. The way I feel the last thing I want to do is dance. Don't you understand anything?

—Don't speak like that to your father, says his former wife.

—Daddy doesn't mind, she says. Do you, Daddy?

B minds everything, though it seems unfatherlike to say so. —If she doesn't want to marry Gregg, he says to her mother, I don't see any reason to try to persuade her otherwise.

—She's already married to Gregg, his ex reminds him. They just had a little lovers' quarrel. It's our job to help them make it up.

—What if she doesn't want to make it up?

—Of course she wants to make it up.

They each look to Sonya for validation of their opposing claims. —I can't stand to watch you fight, she says, sighing. I'm going to go somewhere else. She walks off.

—Why do you think this is fighting, his ex calls after her, and then walks off herself in the same direction. He watches them muddling through the crowd in single file, until they disappear down the

B

aisle that has the Restrooms sign. Before B can trail after them, which is a budding intention, Lisa slide steps in front.

—I've been looking everywhere for you, Mr. B, she says. Dr. Carsik, Gregg's daddy, wants to talk to you man to man. Those are his words, man to man, not mine.

—Why didn't he approach me himself?

—He has this crazy idea that you don't like him, she says.

He doesn't, though he has no idea why the man thinks he knows that. Dr. Carsik appears and holds out his hand to him.

—My friends call me Buddy, he says, squeezing B's hand in a viselike grip.

—What do people who hardly know you call you? he asks.

He waves a scolding finger at B. —You're living up—or is it down?—to your reputation, he says.

Lisa steps between them. —Dr. C would like you to talk to Gregg, she says to him. He thinks Gregg will listen to you.

—This is all Lisa's idea, Buddy says. She has the idea that Gregg admires you because you're some kind of writer. Happens I'm skeptical but anything is possible with Gregg.

2.

Since no one knows where Gregg is at the moment, they go their separate ways to search for him or at least that is the agreed-on plan. In B's private agenda, Gregg is not the primary option. So, indifferent to finding him, he is the first of the searchers to spot Gregg, who is coming out of the Men's Room, sucking on the butt end of a tired cigarette. He considers calling out to him when an attractive woman whom he'd noticed earlier on the dance floor comes up to him.

—You don't remember having met me before, do you? she says. You have, you know.

There is something familiar about her, but he can't come up with a name. —I should know you, he says. Give me a minute.

—I was at your sister-in-law's wedding, she says. You danced with me. I'm a second cousin of your former wife.

—That was a long time ago, he says, reading her narrow interesting face to no avail.

—I was younger then, she says.

An image comes into his head of a seven or eight-year-old child holding out her arms and whirling herself around. He had gone up to her and asked her what she was doing.

—Dancing, she said.

Out of the corner of his eye, he notices Gregg and Sonya talking to each other, their voices hushed, Sonya's hand covering her mouth. He has the sense, evidence to the contrary, that she is crying. No tears are apparent.

—Your name is Anna, he says, the name arriving from wherever unbidden.

—You were so nice to me—that part I can see you don't remember—I was going to warn you not to marry my cousin, she says, her smile unbending. That would have been presumptuous of me, wouldn't it.

—It would have saved me a lot of trouble, he says.

—We all need our trouble, she says.

—Tell me what you've been doing, he says. Bring me up to date.

She laughs at his request. —I haven't done anything that's worth telling about.

—Are you married? he asks.

—Well...yes, she says. Sort of.

—How can you be sort of married? Either you are or you aren't.

—It's not a factor in my life, she says.

Before he can ask her to explain herself, Sonya comes over, Gregg standing (his head turned away) a few feet behind.

—We need to get out of here, Dad, she whispers to him. Could we take your car? I promise we'll bring it back tomorrow.

—So you've made up? he says, secretly disappointed.

—Sort of, she says. Once we get out of here, things are bound to be better.

What can he do but give her the keys and an over elaborate description of where he parked the car. —Do you want to tell me where you're going?

B

She shakes her head.

—We want to go somewhere no one knows about, she says, giving him a quick hug and then scooting away, Gregg in tow. He watches them collect their coats and leave the building, feeling inexplicably heartbroken.

So B doesn't get to dance with his daughter at her wedding.

Anna, who has been standing with her back to him, comes over to mumble something about what a pleasure it was to see him again, which means of course that she also is planning to leave.

—How about a dance before you take off? he says.

She looks at him bemusedly with her mouth partly open as if she were sucking on his offer like a lozenge, looking for the right words to phrase her kind refusal. Then he notices that the music has stopped and the band is packing up its instruments.

—Well, she says. I promised I'd be home by ten o'clock.

—Is this your husband, your sort of husband, you promised?

—Uh huh, she says.

—Perhaps we can share a cab, he says. Which way are you going?

After they collect their coats and walk to the door, Anna says, —I don't think it's such a good idea sharing a cab. Do you mind very much?

—I do, he says. I was looking forward to spending more time with you. But if...

—Then let's do it, she says.

Just as a cab arrives—it takes awhile—B's former wife comes out of the building and calls something to him that sounds like, —This is just like you. Perhaps it is something else, something friendlier.

As soon as the cab takes off, Anna says, —I've been thinking about my own wedding—do you know how it is?—your daughter reminded me of myself. All weddings seem somehow the same wedding. Mine wasn't a big wedding—just some close friends—but it was in a hall bigger than we were at today. As Roland put it, we didn't want it to look as if we were doing something sneaky.

His own memories somehow mingle with hers, though he hangs on her words as she recites her story. He has the impression he is listening to a monologue in a private play.

—Roland is my second husband and I married him a few months after the divorce to Jack was finalized. The thing is, Jack and Roland were partners in a business venture and we got involved while I was still living with Jack. Messy, right? Anyway, I left Jack for Roland because I thought I wouldn't be doing what I was doing unless it was love. You don't want to hear the details. I should mention that Roland was going through his own messy divorce when we got into our thing. We were out on the dance floor at our wedding celebration when it struck me that I was making a mistake in marrying Roland. It was not just that I loved Jack more though I thought that too, but that I needed Jack, needed to be married to Jack, in order to be interested in Roland. This was all going on in my head when Roland, who was a little tipsy, tells me not to expect too much from him. He was being evasive but I knew what he meant. He meant there would be other women on the side, that that was the way he operated. —Remember, it cuts both ways, I said and he said, —Oh God, do I need this, as if I wasn't even there. Something clicked off in me after that and though we got along—Roland's mostly a nice man—the marriage ended for me the day of the wedding.

—But you're still with him, B says. How long has it been?

—Four years, she says, resting her head on his shoulder, but it's never been a real marriage. I've never felt married to him the way I felt married to Jack.

His place is on the way to Anna's so the cab stops for B first. What happens next goes something like this. He presses some money into her hand to cover the cost of the ride, which, after a failed attempt at returning, she hands over to the driver. She refuses her change and follows him out of the cab. Not a word is exchanged until she says, taking his hand, —I'd like to see your place.

He has every intention of inviting her up and letting things take their course. Still, the charm of his memory of her as the precocious little girl he had danced with at a wedding 30 some years back has dissipated during her story in the cab. He continues to find her attractive, but it is his history—perhaps his karma—to avoid complications. He has had enough difficult people in his life.

—You made someone a promise, he reminds her.

—Did I say that? she asks. If I did, I said it to avoid whatever we seem to be getting into now. Roland doesn't care what I do. And what do you care what Roland thinks anyway. You don't even know him.

A cab lets someone out at the building next door and B puts his arm around Anna and urges her gently toward it, opening the door for her with an uncharacteristic grace of gesture that surprises them both.

She takes a moment, apparently puzzled at the turn of events, before climbing into the cab. —Will we ever have our second dance? she asks.

—There's always another time, he says automatically.

—No there isn't, you jerk, she says and pulls the door shut.

He stands at the curb watching the cab disappear around a corner, feeling an unexpected ache of loss—the second this night—aware of being alone in the dark dancing with regret.

XIV. HIS VIEW OF HER VIEW OF HIM

This concerns the day—the hour—the minute—the year—that B finds himself a character in someone else's book, the book sent to him in bound galleys by the author, a woman he was once—what?—intimate with in not easily characterized ways, but hasn't seen in several years. The portrait is not malicious, or not obviously malicious, and is, he supposes, unrecognizable to anyone but himself. Nevertheless it disturbs him as if he had looked into the mirror one day and came upon someone else's deceptively familiar untrustworthy face staring back. His character in the book behaves erratically toward the author's fictional persona, moving close only to pull away, which corresponds roughly to what happened between B and the author in real life. The portrait depresses B because, though accurate in its limited context, it seems at once unrepresentative and deserved.

  The false (accurate) portrait of him in this book makes B want to tell his own story, or at least defend himself against the implied charges against him in the text. What B wants to do is reclaim himself from this caricature version of him that lives briefly on this other author's page.

  The woman had been affectionate and kind—he would allow her her own version of her behavior—and he had been wary and unpredictable. The portrait of him in this woman's book is at once a message to him (see how cowardly you were, the text whispers) and a form of revenge. The truth is, B wanted some kind of sustenance from this woman, wanted to be loved (wanted also not to be loved too much), but didn't want to recapitulate former disastrous patterns. He was coming out of a long term painful marriage with G, whom he had lived with for 16 years (whom he had once much loved) and he was not emotionally ready for what he sensed the woman, who would one day make him into a fictional character, wanted from him.

If he was afraid, which is the way it suited the woman to perceive him, what was at the heart of it? B thinks about it, trying to recall his feelings at the time. In some atavistic pocket of feeling, he tended to equate sex with obligation, a tendency that had led to nothing but grief over the years. Obligation, as he knows it, is the antithesis, the major obstruction, to being his own person. He wants to move in the world without chains of responsibility to anyone but himself.

Above all, he doesn't want to give the woman, or any woman, or anyone for that matter, the wrong impression.

Though his justifications are sincere enough, B suspects that they contain elements of self-deception. His secret motive, a second sense tells him, was revenge. Wounded people behave cruelly despite every good intention to be as kind as desperation allows. After reading of himself in the woman's book, B confides to his journal his own corrective version of what happened between them. Unsatisfied with his own truth (or the piece of it he punishes himself with), B feels compelled to come up with another perspective on the story, one in which the behavior of both characters is more interestingly mysterious. It is not an attempt to justify himself, but to let the events, which are sometimes irrational and confusing, reverberate for themselves.

So when I finally came to accept the fact that my long term now disintegrating marriage to Genevieve was not susceptible to repair, I embarked on a succession of trips as a way of trying out the possibilities of a new life. I visited friends in other cities and countries, accepted residences at writer's colonies, whatever availed to put some distance between me and the woman, my companion for sixteen years, who had become my relentless enemy.

I met Anita at an artist's colony in upstate New York, and for the first week of my stay barely distinguished her from the eight other women in residence. It was not that Anita didn't stand out, it was that my attention was elsewhere. Whenever she looked in my direction she seemed to have a smirk on her face as if we shared an outrageous secret that precluded the others. One night after a dinner when we sat next to each other and made awkward obligatory conversation, I asked her if she'd like to go for a walk. She said she intended to go back to her studio to work, though she accompanied me nevertheless.

What did we talk about? We talked about the other residents, assessed them as if they were difficult texts, while at the same time dropping hints about our own histories. Anita, I learned, had been a concert-level cellist before taking up writing. Her father had died when she was nine. She had a complicated difficult relationship with her mother.

Even then, even after several after-dinner walks, in which pieces of our lives were strewn on the path like debris, I had no clear take on the woman, almost never thought about her when she was out of sight. I tended to obsess about my wife, whose sudden angry disaffection had been greatly puzzling, which meant trying not to obsess about her, which meant trying to shut everything out but the structure of the first paragraph of the novel I had started and restarted and deconstructed several times in the past month.

The embryonic novel, whose first paragraph I was perfecting, concerned a psychotherapist whose much loved wife (also in the shrinking profession) rejects him, and continues to reject him, for no reason he allows himself to understand. My idea was to tell part of the story—half even—from the wife's vantage, inventing a perspective I found mostly incomprehensible as a way of making sense of it.

In the first chapter of the novel, I would tell the story of the marriage from the male protagonist's viewpoint, covering the dynamic of the relationship from their first meeting until the beginnings of the end. The wife's chapter, which would serve as a kind of counter-valence, would deal with things as they were happening and would start later on in the chronology of the novel's events. I sensed that the book had already taken shape inside my head and I had only to open the doors to let it out. My priority at the colony was to get as much of the novel on paper as a four week stay, used unstintingly, might allow.

If I felt written out at the end of the day, I might take a walk with Anita around the grounds or go to the pavilion and play ping-pong with the regulars, but whatever I was doing, my real occupation was in tending the secret emerging novel.

One day, Anita asked me if I could make the time to read her manuscript. She asked in a way that presumed on nothing and allowed for refusal so I said, of course, sure. The manuscript was of an autobiographical episodic novella composed of extremely short self-composed unembellished narratives. I didn't know whether I liked the book—its spareness attracted me—but I saw no reason not to be encouraging. The reading of her text was the beginning of a kind of unsought intimacy. What do I mean by intimacy here? I mean there was something unspoken, something half-conscious and implicitly sexual going on between us. While at the same time there was nothing going on.

When my four week stay was up, I went home to my wife and children, armed with the illusion that my dying marriage might still be revived. I was quickly disabused. I hadn't been home more than a few hours when Genevieve let me know, as she had before, that my presence oppressed her, that there was no hope for us continuing together.

His wife's version of her relationship with B is another story, which means there are three possible narratives here governing the same or related events: the woman's novel, B's counter text, the wife's conjectured story. A fourth text might be introduced here. The story of R, a younger woman B had been seeing off and on during the last years of his marriage. The woman who wrote the book—we'll call her A—has no notion of R, nor has his wife (called G here) who has rejected B while continuing to hold on to him. R, who was in love with B, distrusted him, believed that he would never break with his wife. Even when B separated from G, R continued to think the worst of him. This is background, the rudimentary information necessary to fill in the gaps.

The day before B left for his residence at an artist's colony in New York State, he told R that he didn't want a relationship that excluded seeing others, which precipitated a fight that ended in an agreement—the third or fourth such—to call it quits. Even so, they continued to exchange letters while B was away. Throughout their relationship, R's absence was more compelling to him than her presence. He missed arguing with her over trivialities with life-and-death subtexts, missed their lazy love-making afternoons together. At the colony, A became a substitute for R in the way that R had been a substitute for his disaffected wife.

Can that be right? Was B really behaving as badly as this account makes it seem? That he was in love with the sulky girl, who was 18 years his junior, was his presumptive license to be uncompromising with her. A future with R, as B saw it, would lead inevitably to a slightly varied version of what he had been going through with G. Nothing was worth living that nightmare again, not even illusions of love and renewal. Clearly the long range price was too high.

So B was getting over both wife and mistress when the woman who would one day put him in her book as if his existence were a product of her imagination came into his life. The week before he had asked A for the first time to take an after dinner walk, R had visited, and stayed with B in one of the discreetly decaying Victorian hotels in town. The visit, like most of their times together, had started exuberantly and ended badly, R bitter and accusing, B wanting her gone.

A week or so after B had returned to the city, A called him to say that she was going into the hospital to have an operation to remove a growth from her throat. She joked about it to hide her fear. B joked back, said his wife had just hit him over the head with a gooseneck ed lamp, which also happened to be true. That's terrible, A said laughing, why don't you move out. I'm working on it, he said.

A was back in her Chelsea apartment two days after the operation and called B to let him know of her return. B went over to see her immediately.

Once a week—it was a bit like going to church—B went to divorce mediation with his wife, conducted by a British psychologist in offices near NYU. It reminded him of group therapy, which he looked back on with similar displeasure. Almost all they talked about in divorce mediation was money and property, who got what, and how much he would have to pay his unemployed wife on a monthly basis for the next thirteen years. When the two-hour sessions were over, B visited A at her apartment which was in walking distance from the mediator's office. For B, it was like coming to a safe place after an extended swim in shark-infested waters. He was his usual obsessive self during these visits, replaying the mediation sessions for the woman, as though they were a form of improvisatory theater.

After lunch, they would sometimes sit on the woman's couch and neck, a flirtation that never went beyond the enthusiastic preliminaries. At the colony, one time after walking A to her studio, necking with her outside her door, he was invited in under the proviso that he stay the night after they made love. B reluctantly declined her offer, saying he needed to get a good night's sleep to be able to work in the morning, which was most likely a form of avoidance.

What was at stake in these midday visits? B found the mediation sessions on the near side of unbearable and retreated to A's place for sympathy. He had no idea of his motives beyond blind urge; a fog of need surrounded him. B went to see A because it was pleasant to be with her, and when it stopped being pleasant, when her friendship no longer comforted him, his visits came to an abrupt halt. He had only the most fleeting sense of what A wanted; the dim light he shed on the world at large barely extended beyond his own driven nature. He was putting himself back together—that was the work at hand—by denying to himself he was broken, and it was the kind of work, because so hopeless, that was all encompassing.

B

For all the pleasure he took in A's company, when he was away from her she had no presence in his life. Occasionally, his estranged wife would call, using the pretext of discussing the children to ask for money for one thing or another, using the pretext of asking for money as a means of retaining contact. Everything she did, directly or through the children, overtly unpleasant or insidious, put B in a frantic state.

At some point, to keep his sanity he stopped answering the phone. Sometimes the phone rang as much as twenty-five times, as shrill and persistent as a car alarm. G had to know he was there, avoiding her. Some days he unplugged the phone; other days he left the house to wander the neighborhood visiting friends, stopping at the local greasy spoon for coffee.

For all his evasion and denial, her claim on him seemed inescapable.

Anita was always available when I called, though rarely called herself. In the early months of my separation, what I think of as the first phase, we got together least once a week, usually during the day, more often than not for lunch, a recapitulation of our after-mediation trysts.

She sometimes asked why I didn't see her in the evenings or perhaps that was Rebecca and I'm confusing the two.

Rebecca was on a brown rice and tofu diet, Anita was smoking nicotine-free cigarettes and drinking alcohol-free beer. Both women were into selective forms of exclusion, which seemed to me a worrisome principle. They were practicing to do without. Was I next on their denial agenda?

While they were paring down their lives, I was into unselective inclusion, wanting something and accepting anything. I meant no harm or meant perhaps—in some unseen way—only harm.

So I visited Anita no more than once a week for lunch or dinner, usually at one of the local ethnicities—the Thai restaurant, or the Afghan, or the Mexican or the red sauce Italian with the checkered tablecloths covered in see-through plastic, never staying overnight though never foreclosing the possibility.

I tended to see Rebecca either not at all or three times a week in her TriBecca loft, discussing commitment or my lack thereof, eating and being eaten, wooing (the wooing our most passionate act), and fucking, going home forlorn at two every morning convinced that this time it was irrevocably over.

Then there was Jane, who I haven't mentioned before, an old flame, who I met once every two weeks for dinner. We were each other's confidantes—in some ways a more intense intimacy than sex—and I discussed things with Jane about Rebecca, Genevieve and Anita I had mentioned to no one else. We were the other's main source of support, which sometimes led to extended hugs, which in turn led (how imposingly intimate our conversations) to barely resistible desire.

We flirted with the possibility—it was always there like a subtext—of becoming lovers again, and every once in a while, usually after a few drinks, one of us would make a move toward the other. What do you think? one of us would say. What do you want to do? was the answer. What do you want to do? was the answer's echo. By that time, the sense of urgency had abated. We danced on the precipice of trespass and one of us, not always the same one, would always pull back at the last moment. That it hadn't happened didn't rule out that it might happen eventually.

B tends to lose sight of his subject, which in this case is A, the woman who employed him as an unnamed character in her book. She seems overjoyed to see him when he arrives at her apartment, a corner of the mouth smirk on her face, an unlisted smile with an underground subtext—a smile which says to him, Your secret whatever is mine, and mine whatever is yours. B wonders where such presumed knowledge comes from.

When they walk together in the city streets, A takes his arm, hooks her hand under his arm in a casually possessive manner. She has caught him, madness tells him, he will never get away.

It troubles B that he has unwittingly given the woman the

wrong impression concerning his intentions, which are a coded text indecipherable even to himself. It's also possible that A has willfully misread him. She tends to show inappropriate, as he sees it, pleasure on his arrival at her place, her insinuating smile in full blossom, which is at once gratifying and frightening. Whatever it is she imagines herself to want from him is clearly more than he is prepared to give.

Whatever is going on remains on her part insidiously implicit. This is not something he can say to her over lunch at the Hunan Adventure or even afterward when they are in her apartment and she is praising one of his books or making coffee for him in her espresso pot. To say any of the things he is feeling would be presumptuous on his part and not a little insulting so of course he says nothing.

He can't tell her that as much as he enjoys her company he also wants to get away, wants to get away and never return. That is one of the secrets he has that, despite her knowing manner, she is unable or unwilling to penetrate. B is in constant imaginative flight from the encroachments of intimacy.

The truth is, A makes no overt demands on him, doesn't complain about the conflicting signals he offers. Her demands, which he imagines to be extensive, remain unannounced. She wants the unimaginable from him, and deceives him by asking for nothing. It is her slyness that concerns B, it is her slyness that sets off alarms, that sparks an instinctive wariness.

B moves in and out of A's life as though she were a novel he was reading he had put down and picked up and put down again. He values the book most when it is out of his hands, when it is on the verge of being lost. A is almost always available to see him when he calls, she never (like some others) complains of the vagaries of his comings and goings. She understands and forgives, perhaps even dotes on, his bad behavior. She's seen it all before.

One time he dropped in on A without calling first only to discover she had another date. She was apologetic, though of course had no reason to be, offered to let him stay at her place while she was gone, insisting she would return in a few hours. B declined her offer and went off to a movie by himself.

Afterward, calling first, he dropped in on R whom he hadn't

seen in almost a month, and they argued into the early hours mostly about his behavior, about which R was unsparingly critical. When he gave up defending himself and made ready to leave, R became forlorn, apologized for her "brattiness" and threw herself on him, pleading with him to stay, pressing herself against him.

I hated it when Rebecca became frantic and demanding because it ultimately compromised us both. If I yielded to her as I mostly did, I tended to feel manipulated afterward and consequently angry at us both. If I resisted her pleading and carried through my initial intention, which usually meant leaving her to go home, I would feel equally bad for being the occasion of her pain. I took no pleasure in the gratuitous power her vulnerability acceded to me. I felt responsible for Rebecca, which made me want to run from her all the more.

And yet I couldn't stay away, couldn't stand not to see her for prolonged periods of time. Something about her touched me deeply. When she wasn't complaining or frantic, she could be charming and precocious in her girlish way—the smartest and sexiest child of 28 imaginable. I couldn't stay away from her and, when with her, I couldn't get away fast enough.

We were driving each other crazy and I didn't know how to break the pattern.

Jane advised me in her unassertive way to stop seeing Rebecca, said it seemed to her that things would only get worse. We were in her living room at the time, sitting apart on her striped Salvation Army couch, trading confidences. I defended Rebecca to her, said she was not as crazy as I made her seem.

—She's probably worse, Jane said, but you don't want to stop so you won't.

I had recently stopped therapy and my conversations with Jane became an unwitting replacement.

The next day, with the intention of breaking up with Rebecca, I called her and asked her to meet me for lunch at a restaurant near her loft.

B

—I can't, she said. I really don't want to see you any more. Okay? Okay?

I might have accepted her verdict and got off the phone but instead I said, —Don't you think we ought to discuss this in person?

—I want to end it just like this, she said, okay?, and then, allowing me two heartbeats of unspoken response, hung up.

My first impulse was to congratulate myself at having gotten out of this mess so bloodlessly. My second was to call her back and demand an explanation. My third impulse was to appear at her door and tell her that I realized I loved her and would see her from now on on her terms, which is to say to the exclusion of other women. I imagined taking her to bed as if it were again the first time. The pleasure, as always—as sometimes—was intoxicating. I played scenario three out in the imagination from first act to last talking my way through the door, gradually appeasing her tactical resistance, holding her hand, listening to her music, dancing with her, going down on her, fucking her, lying with her in her bed, fucking her again. And then afterward the old bitterness on her part surfacing, the free-floating jealousy, the claims of grief and despair.

The imagined scenario foreclosed the possibility of a real one. Having played out my options, I was content to let matters stand as they were. I made no attempt to get back in touch with Rebecca. I felt disburdened.

Following my pattern, which was to move from one woman to another, I arranged to see Anita that evening. At first I was glad to see her–how reasonable she seemed compared to sulky Rebecca— but then my pleasure in her company began to fade. It was as if whatever we were doing—talking, hugging, sharing a meal—we had done before and done more interestingly before. I made some excuse to leave early (said I wasn't feeling well) and went home. Anita gave me a homeopathic medicine called Echinacea to take along—she said it had cured a friend who had been given up for dead—and I somehow managed, after putting the bottle of pills in my jacket pocket, to come away without it.

When I got home I discovered I really wasn't feeling well and took a couple of aspirin and, though it was only 10 o'clock, got out of my clothes and went to bed. The phone woke me at three a.m. and I struggled to get out of bed—I was feverish and my legs ached—to reach the phone in time. I thought I answered (it was someone speaking Spanish), but it turned out to be a dream. I never got out of bed.

In the morning I staggered about the house looking for a thermometer, which I vaguely remembered seeing somewhere or other, in the night table drawer or in the medicine cabinet, the image of its presence precise and variable. Not finding it in its place, I wrapped myself in my covers and went back to sleep.

Again the ringing of the phone woke me. I was surprised to find Rebecca on the line and the conversation, which was actual, turned out to be more dreamlike than the one I had in my dream in the middle of the night.

—I've missed you, she said in her childish sing-song. I want you to come and see me if that's what you want.

—I'm sick, I said. I don't have the strength to get out of bed. A silence followed in which I sensed her assessing my claim. —I'm so sorry, she said. Are you sick sick?

Her question puzzled me, seemed in my feverish state to contain its own echo. —I can't find the thermometer so it's hard to say.

She laughed nervously. —You're not putting me on, are you? You're truly sick? You sound sick to me.

I was shivering and in reaching for the covers, which I meant to throw over my shoulders, I dropped the phone. When I recovered it, which was mostly a slow-motion operation, Rebecca was gone. I crawled back under the covers and yielded to the spell of my fever, slipped into dreams no more preposterous than the phone call I had to rehearse in my mind not to forget.

Two hours later, feeling a little better, I phoned Rebecca as a kind of reality check. —Did you call a while ago? I asked her.

—When? she asked in a wary voice.

—Then I must have dreamed your call, I said. I'm sorry I bothered you. Though strange, it was extremely real.

—Why did you hang up on me?

—You're giving yourself away, I said. I didn't hang up on you.

B

I dropped the phone.

She cackled. –If I believe that, I'll believe anything, right? Would you like me to bring you some chicken soup? I could also bring a thermometer if you haven't found yours.

–Okay, I said.

–*Tout al'heure*, she said.

I was feeling a little better after that—the promise of being looked after sufficed for the thing itself—and I got dressed and went downstairs and had some breakfast. When Rebecca appeared two hours later with an overnight bag and a brown bag of wholistic health-food groceries, prepared to nurse me through a long illness, I was sitting at my computer, working on my novel.

I found her nursing mode unaccountably attractive, and I put my arms around her sinuous frame, but she slipped away to get her thermometer. She was as always single-minded. She had come to visit my illness, to play with it and improve its disposition, and would not be distracted by concerns outside her immediate agenda. I was obliged to play sick for her, gave myself over to her uncompromising ministrations. Her thermometer ravished the delicate membranes under my tongue. My temperature was disappointing, barely over a hundred, my illness a contemptibly small thing, unworthy of the sacrifice she had come to make.

–You may be someone who doesn't run a high fever, she said, making excuses for me to cover over her disappointment, yes? I nodded ambiguously. Tea came next, fortified with honey and lemon juice, followed by chicken broth, which I took sitting up in bed, pillow fluffed behind me, trying to be a patient worthy of her commitment to heal.

B's friends, men and women alike, tended to invite him to dinner parties in which there were unattached women in assemblage, the impulse entrepreneurial and generous, perhaps even authorial. B did the correct thing at evening's end and escorted the women home, the ones who didn't live too far out of his way, the ones who didn't have their own transportation. That's how he met V, who had been widowed barely a year ago, and was invited to dinner by mutual friends to meet B. At this point B had recently broken up with R and had been seeing A (the woman who would one day fictionalize him) with increasing irregularity and so he saw himself as relatively unattached.

When V invited him up for a drink, B hesitated before accepting. It was already past midnight and he had a long drive home. He saw himself as being open to whatever came next, whatever the situation offered, nothing foreclosed in advance, so he went up to see what about V her apartment revealed, promising himself in advance not to stay more than an hour. Unlike A and R and to some extent even J, V lived like an adult, had an ample apartment with furniture that had not been picked off the street or bought on sale at the Door Store.

V offered him a brandy which he declined, opting instead for club soda or water, and they talked about nothing much for a while, enlarged small talk, facing each other in her showcase living room, couch to arm chair, and then he went home.

The next day, the woman who had invited them to dinner called to ask if he had left a blue cashmere-blend scarf at her apartment. In the course of the conversation, she asked, not wanting to pry of course, how he had gotten on with V.

—I liked her, he said.

—That's a diplomatic answer, the woman said. So it didn't go so well, I suppose. It may be too soon for her, you know what I mean. Or maybe it's too soon for you. Something like that.

B saw no reason to be evasive. —I think we liked each other, he said.

After the mutual friend hung up, while B was considering what he wanted to do in respect to V, A called and invited him to dinner that night. It was rare for her to call, which gave the invitation a certain authority it might not otherwise have had, and B, who had every intention of accepting, found himself saying that he had a prior commitment. That's when he called V and asked her to have dinner with him. V said, groaning, that she couldn't, she was sorry, then she said, before B could say he was sorry too, that she would see what she could do about getting out of her other commitment, which was really not firm, and call him back.

B ended up going to V's house for dinner that night, which was the night after he had taken V home from the party, and therefore sooner than might seem appropriate without giving, or seeming to give, the impression that he was pursuing her. Expect nothing from me, he felt obliged to say, but delivered the message implicitly instead through imperceptible gesture.

This account is not about B's relation to V, is only about it in regard to how it impacts on his relation to A. At least a month passed before B had communication with A again, A initiating the communication as she had the time before, catching him at home one evening while cooking dinner for his sons.

As soon as I was indisputably well, which was two days later, Rebecca put her thermometer in its case and announced it was time to return home. There was something about the announcement that asked, virtually pleaded, for further negotiation. I thanked her for looking after me, sought out her mouth to kiss her good-bye.

–I didn't do it to be thanked, she said, lips in a pout, face turned away.

I had said the wrong thing but what could I say to make things right–what was it she wanted to hear? –Why did you do it? I asked.

–Because I care about you, she snapped.

–If you care about me, I said, why are you so angry at me?

–I'm angry at you because you don't know why I'm angry at you, she said. I'm not really angry, I'm disappointed. To thank me is the most inappropriate and insensitive thing you could possibly do. Invisible flames emanated from her on all sides.

–You're beautiful when you're impossible, I said.

Rebecca almost smiled. –Anyway I have to go, she said. I've overstayed my welcome. And she was gone.

I walked her to the subway, bought her a token.

–You're glad to see me go, aren't you? she said.

I didn't deny it. No gracious half-truth, no credible lie, passed my lips. —I'm also sorry to see you go, I said.

After passing through the turnstile, she turned and called back to me. —Take care of yourself, she stage-whispered in a voice that turned heads. Next time you get sick, you might not find anyone to look after you.

About a month after V entered B's life, he stopped seeing virtually all the other women that filled his days, including A, his free time consumed by the new relationship. V, as I said before, is not the issue here, nor is G, to whom he was still married, nor is J, nor is R. Some time later, A showed up at a reading B was giving in a Soho gallery, made her presence felt by sitting in the center of the first row. Her insistent presence—V was also there—made B uncomfortable. It was as if she had some prior claim on him and had come to his reading to make him aware that she had no intention of stepping aside. He did what he could to disguise his panic, said hello to A, though his manner was distant and he sensed that she was hurt by it.

He phoned her the next day to apologize but got her answering service and left no message.

After that, A would call from time to time at odd hours, with odd sometimes unlikely requests. Sometimes she called without explanation and they chatted awkwardly, usually about something in A's life, a horrific meeting with a former husband, a fight she had with her mother, a choice she had to make between two job offers. Though sometimes her calls interrupted his work, he never cut her off, let the conversation go on for as long as it suited her. It was as though he owed her something—kindness at the very least—though he could not say why, could not put his sense of obligation to her into words. He simply put himself at her disposal during these calls because that was what he could do for her. He didn't welcome these calls, though he didn't not welcome them either, didn't try to evade them as he did his wife's.

It was in the way of things that A would call every once in a while, her tone always a little ironic, the same presuming smirk in her voice that she had in her glance when he met her at the writer's

B

colony years back.

Sometimes two months passed between calls, sometimes six, sometimes over a year. They never discussed him in these talks—she had done listening to him years ago, was tired of hearing him complain about his former wife's unfairness—but dealt solely with her issues. At times, the calls were merely requests for favors—recommendations for jobs or fellowships, blurbs for forthcoming books—which, no matter how busy he was with other commitments, he always granted without hesitation.

The calls continued without discernible pattern. Although no arrangements were made for getting together, he would run into her from time to time usually at a place that he was more likely to be than she. If these meetings were not the coincidence they appeared, it was not something he thought about with concern.

One day, unable to sleep, he found himself staring out the living room window, surprised to discover a car double-parked in front of his house, a shadowy figure sitting in the driver's seat, hunched forward over the wheel.

I began increasingly to value my privacy during this transitional period in my life. What do I mean by that? The truth is, I was hiding out, avoiding emotional creditors.

The phone rang two or three times an hour, but I had an answering machine (with a message I changed every few hours) to represent me in my self-imposed exile. Sometimes I erased the day's messages without even screening them—more often I listened to them with a glass of wine in my hand before erasing them.

I answered some of my calls, though not always right away, not always the next day or the day after, in no hurry to hear the voice of accusation in its righteous heat. Rebecca and Genevieve, in fluctuating order, were the ones who called most often, averaging between them about 10 calls a week. In third place was the caller (or several callers)—I made no suppositions—who left only silent messages. These usually came after midnight. I imagined some of the silent calls came from Anita, though I had no evidence for that assumption. For about a two month's period, except on inescapable occasions, I lived my life without the company of women. What was the point? you might ask. Was I happier without women? No, I wasn't. What I was was less burdened by unanswerable demands.

This was about the time I was invited by the Femmes Club to give a talk on the parameters of marriage at the Fort Hamilton Armory.

B was alone in the house and the double-parked car, a black, late-model, mid-sized American, with a shadowy driver folded over the wheel like some coiled snake, made him uneasy. He found an aluminum baseball bat in the closet of his younger son's room and, after a few practice swings, he took it to bed with him, slept alongside it in case the figure in the car, or some unseen other, intended him harm. Though it seemed unimaginable, he couldn't help reflect on the extremely remote possibility that a contract had been taken out on his life.

When the phone rang—it was not yet morning—instead of answering, he went to the front window to see if the black car was still on vigil in front of the house. That the car was gone made him easier about returning to sleep. He expected no message from his caller and received none.

A crashing sound coming from inside the house woke him. He listened to the sound echo in memory and placed it on the third floor almost directly overhead. Before leaving his bed, he waited in vain for further indications of an intruder.

Carrying the bat in readiness as if he might be called on to pinch hit, B investigated the third floor. A painting had fallen from the wall of one of his son's bedrooms. It was an explanation, if an unsatisfying one, for the frightening crash that had exploded him from sleep.

Later in the day, after adding two sentences to the possible final chapter of his novel, B called V at work to confide his irrational fears.

—No one wants to kill you, she assured him. I take that back.

B

It is unlikely in the extreme that anyone is both angry enough and crazy enough to pay good money to have you killed.

B was convinced and at the same time unable to let go of his obsession, which stuck in him like a burr. —G wants to kill me, he said.

V laughed. —Yes, but she doesn't need a gun to do the job.

That evening, waiting for V in front of a Japanese restaurant in the theater district, B noticed A idling by in a preoccupied state on the other side of the street. She appeared to be unaware of him and he was about to call to her when he decided instead to avoid her by standing behind a tree. At this point V arrived and they kissed in front of the restaurant, an extended greeting, B glancing over V's shoulder and meeting A's eyes.

That was the first time he was aware that there was a previously unchartered pain in his left hip

I had no reason to believe that Anita was following me beyond two perhaps three circumstantial meetings. When an episode in your life ends inconclusively, you tend, in writing about it, to let the story devise its own next step. Anita's next step was to put me in her book in an anonymous way as one of the vexing shadows in her life. As I was her shadow, she had become mine.

What did she hope to gain by sending me a copy of her book with the unflattering portrait of me in it? Was I supposed to respond? Was it the opening of a new dialogue between us?

Recently, I looked for her book on my shelf to see again what it was she had written about me, and I couldn't find it. The book had mysteriously walked away, or more to the point, I had put it somewhere unattainable.

There are reductive questions to be asked and B feels obliged to ask them whenever feelings of mortality arrive unannounced. What's it all about, he asks himself, this frantic waking dream between birth and death? Answers will reveal themselves eventually, he believes—he has absolute wavering faith that they will. That's why his appearance in A's book at first had certain positive aspects for him. Well, B thought, maybe A knew something about him, had some special insight that would show him to himself in a new light.

Though somewhat wary of the prospect, he was prepared to see himself in a new light, to discover some unacknowledged secret self, through her eyes. As it turned out, A only knew him from the limited vantage of how his presence in her life had impact on her self-concern. He was a man who had failed her. The character that apparently represented him was an unnamed older man toward whom she was inexplicably drawn, someone, who for reasons of fearfulness, had only fitfully returned her affection. That was the sum of his sketchy identity in the dream pages of her book.

A's portrait of B did not yield much in the way of his understanding of self. He was a fantasy figure for A, whose interest was less in his character than in how his disappointing behavior was congruent with the disappointing behavior of other men in her fictionalized life.

Some months have passed since he's read A's book and his memory of the passages that apparently refer to him have receded into vagueness.

I have all of Anita's books on my shelf except the one in which I appear, which remains, despite my obsessive search for it everywhere, persistently unavailable. The book's inexplicable absence enhances its mystery. I go around to a few local book stores only to discover that the disappeared book, which is called *Fathers*, has been sold out or, as in one case, never put on order. Other matters in my life supplant the obsession with Anita's text and I forget my quest while going on, as is my pattern, to some new feckless pursuit.

Then one day, wandering about in Books & Co., looking for a gift for my father, I discover *Fathers* staring at me from its alphabetized perch in the Psychology section of the store. Wasn't it written as fiction? Has it been misshelved or is it possible that I've misperceived its nature all along?

B picks up the copy of the woman's book—the last available, the only one—from its home on the bookstore shelf and riffles through the pages, trying without success to find the references to him that had been so upsetting on first encounter. He leans against a wall and reads the first thirty-two pages of the book. He is a missing person, a manifest absence, an effaced self. If, as fading memory insists, he is a character in the book, he must nevertheless occupy a very small portion of its pages. He scans the last twelve pages. When he looks up from the text, he notices that several people are watching him. Self-consciousness distracts him and after reading the closing section, he puts the book back on the shelf. Is it possible (reason suggests not) that the copy sent to him by the author has an altered text meant only for his eyes?

I walk away from *Fathers*, leave the book behind as I have, I suppose, left Anita herself behind, and return to my bookshelves at home. The author's presence, though dimly felt, survives for me in her other books. Like her texts, Anita, as I call her here, is sardonic, whimsical, deadpan, angry at the betrayal of fathers and father surrogates, a chronicler of disappointed survival. I am just another disappointing shadow-father in the life she imagines for herself as fiction. Doesn't it also follow that I have been a shadow, though a somewhat different one in each case, in the lives of Rebecca, Jane and Genevieve as well?

I am the father, the surrogate father, the false shadow of the father, who has already betrayed them irrevocably. My part in their story has been written in advance. I am crowned only to be deposed, trusted only to betray that trust, adored only to be despised and rejected.

Putting it all in perspective, B recognizes that at best he is just another negligible player in the writer A's fictional memoir. Perhaps he is not even that, perhaps he is only there by dint of imaginative leap.

It is a presumption, after all, to imagine oneself someone else's character. There are several male characters in A's text, one of whom (none of whom) may be a stand-in for B. B, who conceives himself a presence in another's book, is at this moment sitting in front of his computer inventing the text that appears above under the author's real name. A is just a construct in the text, an occasion for its invention. She is only real (as is her book containing B) within these pages, which is also true of the others, the wife G, the young mistress R, the confidante J, V the new woman in his life, and also of course B himself, the hero of the text, the author's invented self.

—

Turn the page and we all fall away into the ether like matter converting itself into traces of smoke, like the elegy of forgotten dreams.

Born in Brooklyn, son of a painter, father of four including a filmmaker, Jonathan Baumbach is the author of numerous books, including *Reruns, Babble, Chez Charlotte & Emily, The Life and Times of Major Fiction, Seven Wives* and *D-Tours*. Though mainly a novelist, he has published over 80 short stories in such places as *Esquire, American Review, Fiction International, Partisan Review* and *TriQuarterly*. He has been widely anthologized and has appeared in *O.Henry Prize Stories* and *Best American Short Stories*. In 1973, he cofounded Fiction Collective, the first large scale writing cooperative in America. He has written on movies for *Partisan Review* and is a former chairman of the National Society of Film Critics. Over the years, he has taught at Brooklyn College, Brown, Princeton, NYU, Columbia, Tufts, University of Washington and Ohio State. He currently lives in Brooklyn, N.Y. and Great Barrington, Mass.